A native of Mich
New York, where
video businesses
writing . . . and in New Mexico, where she wrote her
previous novel, *Star Gazer*.

Having continued her westward migration, she now lives in Los Angeles, where she is again working in the record business and currently writing her third novel featuring Dr Mackenzie Griffin.

Also by Jeanne McCafferty

Star Gazer

Artist Unknown

Jeanne McCafferty

First published in 1995 by
HEADLINE BOOK PUBLISHING

First published in paperback in 1996 by
HEADLINE BOOK PUBLISHING

A HEADLINE FEATURE paperback

10 9 8 7 6 5 4 3 2 1

ISBN 0 7472 5087 1

Typeset by Avon Dataset Ltd, Bidford-on-Avon, Warks

Printed and bound in Great Britain by
Mackays of Chatham PLC, Chatham, Kent

HEADLINE BOOK PUBLISHING
A division of Hodder Headline PLC
338 Euston Road
London NW1 3BH

Dedicated, with affection and respect, to teachers whose paths I have been fortunate enough to cross in this life:

members of two extraordinary communities of women, the Adrian Dominican Sisters of Adrian, Michigan, and the Religious of the Sacred Heart of Mary of Tarrytown, New York;

two gentlemen whose intelligence and humor have resonated in my life long after the actual classes ended, Frederick S. Strath and Ronald M. Weyand;

and, of course, Noella Finn Laube, teacher in my youth and friend for a lifetime.

ACKNOWLEDGEMENTS

My thanks:

To Brian McCafferty, whose eye and pen are as sharp as
ever, and who did a splendid job (as usual) in cleaning
up the first draft;

To Julia McLaughlin, for her early reading and helpful
comments, and especially for her insights into the
world and language of art historians;

To Gregory LaChapelle, for his encouragement (in more
ways than one);

To Robin McCafferty, for her assistance in compiling
the research;

To Barrymore Laurence Scherer, for his helpful
suggestions on names;

To John T. Greene, for his continuing assistance on
information concerning John Jay college and the City
University of New York;

To the reference librarians of the Wyoming Regional
Branch of the Albuquerque Public Library, for their
patient assistance;

To Leonard J. Charney, for his continuing enthusiasm,
and to Wendy Schmalz, for her continuing patience;

And finally, to Kay Davis and her colleagues in the MoP
for providing, when most needed and appreciated, the
wind beneath my wings.

ONE

At least until the shot rang out, the beach was quiet and empty – just the way Mac liked it. That was one of the joys of walking the beach in the spring, or the winter, or, like now, in the fall. Anytime, actually, other than summer. Sun-worshippers have no idea of the beauty of the beach in autumn.

Like the way it looked now. It was only the second of November, but somehow the sky already reflected the change in the month. Last weekend, even back in Manhattan, the sky had been a brilliant October blue. But now, looking out toward where Long Island Sound met Block Island Sound, and beyond that, to where the vast body of water suddenly became the Atlantic Ocean, the gray water was met by a lighter gray sky, and it took concentration to see the line where one became the other. There would still be a few bursts of clear autumn sky, but the gray that was New England in the winter was obviously settling in.

But the gray of the water and the sky also created a clear light. In that clear, flat light the sand of the beach, sprinkled here and there with the orange and red and yellow leaves of the nearby trees, combined with the seaweed, twigs and shells that delineated the tide line to create a visual tone-poem of neutrals. Add to the picture the colors of the large rocks – boulders, really – that Mac was scrambling across, and you had a timeless landscape.

The scene was made all the better by the quiet. There was no wave action at all today; the Sound was as placid as a swimming pool. Mac could hear her own footsteps scrunch in the sand, and the light nylon windbreaker she wore emitted its own little whistle as the sleeves rubbed against the body of the jacket.

The quiet was occasionally shattered by the honking of the swans or the scream of a seagull. Or by the plop! that one of the shellfish made as it was dropped from on high by a gull preparing for dinner. It was amazing to watch the precision of the birds. A gull would fly over the section of the beach that was covered with melon-sized rocks, drop the shell it had been carrying in its mouth, continue on its course, then curve around, swoop down, and return to the exact two-inch-square spot where that fresh morsel of seafood awaited it.

Once she skirted the next nest of boulders, Mac picked up the pace again as she came to a hard flat stretch of sand. She wanted to get her blood pumping; even with sweat pants on, and the windbreaker over a long-sleeved T-shirt, she still felt chilly in the damp air.

It had been good to get out of the city this weekend. Actually, she'd made it up to Registon by Thursday night, since this was the beginning of a mid-semester break at school. The primary reason for her coming up this weekend, despite her mother's notion that she'd come up to attend the

Riverside University fund-raiser, was to help her brother Chad get settled.

Chad had bought one of the local art galleries – had just closed on the sale the other day, as a matter of fact – and he was back in Registon for good, or so he said. Mac had her doubts about Chad living in their parents' home – even temporarily – after living on his own for eight years. Actually, she had doubts about his living back in Registon (population 4,835) after two years in New York and then five in Washington, DC. But even if she wasn't entirely persuaded of the wisdom of his decision, Mac decided to show her support for her brother in the way she knew best – by helping.

Of course he'd have been able to do everything himself, but Mac was ever the big sister. Chad was only three years younger that she, but Mac had sort of taken over the care and feeding of her siblings when she was about twelve, and even twenty years later she still hadn't been able to break the habit. 'Codependent behavior,' Peter had called it. 'Pop psychology in the hands of amateurs,' Mac had replied.

That was another reason she was glad to be out of the city this weekend. Peter was in Tokyo. Or maybe he was in Osaka by now, she wasn't sure; trying to figure out the time and date difference had made her crazy. At any rate, he was on tour in New Zealand, Australia, and some cities in Asia, and even though he'd been gone only since the beginning of the week Mac missed him already.

Mac had met Peter Rossellini in the late spring, when she was called in to consult on a police case that involved him. In the year prior, Peter had emerged as America's newest pop music star, and, unfortunately, someone had started using his music videos as blueprints for murder. Early in the investigation, Peter had made it clear that he was attracted to Mac, but she begged off on any kind of personal involvement until the case was wrapped up.

The video-inspired murderer had been caught, with Mac's assistance, but Peter had left on a national tour almost immediately, so they were left to deal with what was obviously a mutual attraction over long distance lines. From early June through the end of August, what they did was talk. At first Peter called her two or three times a week, then every day from wherever he was across the US. The friendship that was formed over those weeks of conversation moved rather easily into a 'relationship' once Peter returned the week before Labor Day.

Their relationship (a buzz word which Mac had come to loathe) was a surprise to both her friends and his. After all, what in the world could they have in common? But Mac's theory was that their worlds were so different, each found the other's totally intriguing. Peter was enthralled by Mac's daily accounts of life at John Jay College of Criminal Justice, where the courses she taught in criminal psychology and the seminars she led for professionals in the justice system attracted police officers, corrections officials, academics and social workers (among others) as students. The black and white reality of that world fascinated Peter.

Mac was amazed by the unexpected discipline that Peter's life in the entertainment world required. His touring show, which took a little less than two hours in performance, was, in fact, a twenty-four hour commitment for a number of

4

people. She was astounded by the staggering amount of work that went in to making the show look effortless. And Mac loved listening to Peter's usually funny and sometimes bawdy stories (which he was *very* good at telling) about the musicians and the singers, the record company executives and the roadies. Peter's world was a technicolor escape for Mac.

They concluded that their worlds intersected, however, in the everyday politics of people working together. Academia and show business, it turned out, weren't all that far apart.

Since September, virtually all their social time was spent quite happily in each other's company, and this was the first time since then that Mac had gone days without seeing him. And she missed him. Which is why this weekend visit had seemed like a good idea.

Chad and Mac had gotten nearly all his things settled in the house by Friday afternoon, and they were able to spend most of this morning in his new gallery. The building itself was in pretty good shape: two exhibition rooms, an office and a storeroom. The interior was immaculate; Malcolm Howard, the retiring dealer from whom Chad had bought the River's End Gallery, was a fastidious man, and that fastidiousness showed in the care of the building. The woods were highly polished, the windows gleamed, and not even the skirting boards showed a speck of dust. The exterior needed a little work, especially around the window frames, and come spring Chad would have to get somebody in to re-do the landscaping. But it was a great location, not far from the Boston Post Road, and Chad was excited about having his own place at last. After lunch, they'd experimented with

5

different furniture arrangements in the small office; by the time they called it quits it was only 2:30, and Mac had decided she had time to run home, change her clothes, and go for one of her long walks on the beach.

The sound of a motor caught her attention, and she turned around. This chunk of beach that she was walking sat just to the east of where the Connecticut River emptied into Long Island Sound, and the engine she'd heard was that of a barge just coming off the river and turning west into the Sound. The barge was probably a quarter of a mile away from her, but the shape of the water and the land, aided by the eerie absence of sound as the water lapped at the sand, had created a strange acoustical environment, and this engine sounded like it was within feet of her.

Mac watched the boat for a moment, and noticed how quickly the sound diminished as the craft moved toward Old Saybrook. When the engine had first caught her attention, she was just about to start the trek over another rock field. It was difficult walking, and demanded absolute attention to each step. Before starting across, she decided to take advantage of the flat sand where she stood now and take in the view.

Her eyes skimmed the horizon from the right, past the Saybrook Point lighthouse, then across to Long Island. The cold November light made it possible to see the outline of some large trees over near Orient Point, the northernmost part of Long Island, some ten miles away. As she continued scanning the horizon, Mac was surprised to see a cabin cruiser out on the water to the left, toward Block Island. She didn't remember seeing the boat when she'd glanced this way before. The boating season was fairly short in New England, and you rarely saw pleasure craft in the water this late in the year. Mac wasn't good at identifying boats, but this one looked like a good-sized, double-decked cruiser. She was also not good at estimating distances over water, so she couldn't judge how far out it was, but it was pretty tiny to look at, so it was out a ways. It didn't seem to be moving, either. These people must be new to New England, she thought. Didn't they know how fickle the weather was? That it could be forty-five one day, like it was today, and suddenly below freezing the next? One quick November snowstorm and maybe then they'd realize why most everyone tucked their boats away by the end of September.

Mac turned and started picking her way across the rocks. This section of the beach didn't make it easy to maintain any kind of aerobic pace in walking, but it sure helped improve eye-foot coordination and balance. Even after the eye had picked out what seemed a reasonable rock to step on, the foot would suddenly feel the slippery surface, or perhaps the sand would shift underneath. When she was a child, Mac started pretending she was a high-wire artist from the circus, and she would hold her arms out just like one of those performers would. That's exactly what she did now. That's what helped her keep her balance when the shot rang out.

At least it sounded like a shot – that strange whine that a bullet makes when it passes through the chamber and into the air. Mac had to concentrate on righting herself, and she quickly made it to the other side of the rock field so she could look around and see where that sound had come from. There were some homes not far from the beach at this point, but she looked up the dune and across the grass to where the cluster of three homes sat. Nothing. No one.

She turned and looked up and down the horizon again. She couldn't see anything but the cruiser, but given that distance it was hard to believe the sound had come from that far off. It had sounded close enough to her that her instinct had been to duck, which was why maintaining her balance had been such a problem.

Maybe her ears were playing tricks on her again. Hard to tell, given what the atmosphere was doing to sound waves today. Her heart was racing a bit, and she breathed deeply to get it back into rhythm again. Still staring out over the water, her eye caught a little movement over on the cruiser. It was far away, and Mac squinted to try and sharpen her vision. Not much help. She thought she could see a man – a person – moving around the back of the craft, but she really couldn't tell. Then she thought she saw something – a good-sized something, dark and bigger, say, than a full garbage bag – go over the back end of the boat into the water.

Her heart was getting back to normal, but Mac still stood there, watching, wishing that her eyes would suddenly become like – who was it? Wonder Woman? No, the Bionic Woman. No, she was the one who had the good ear. Maybe it was Superman. Yes, she wanted Superman's eyes so she could see exactly what was going on out there on the water. She heard an engine start up suddenly, loudly, and had no doubt of the source of the noise this time. Within moments, the cruiser she'd been watching was moving, and moving quickly, turning a sharp curve and heading east toward Block Island Sound.

Mac stood exactly where she was for long moments, trying to think through this situation. On the one hand, there was a possibility that she'd just heard someone get shot, and she'd just seen the body dumped. On the other hand, she may have heard a backfire and seen somebody dumping garbage off the back of his boat. Illegal and tacky, and certainly not environmentally correct, but a long way from murder.

So what was real? And what was imagination running wild? Was her work getting to her? Would someone other than a teacher of criminal psychology have the same reaction she did?

She imagined going into the chief's office and reporting it. Until the year before last, Registon, like many of the small towns in Connecticut, had part-time police officers who took care of many of the routine matters of public safety. Actual crimes were investigated by the state police, and there was a resident trooper in town. Then the town council had decided two years ago that there were sufficient funds in the budget to allow for a full-time, two-and-a-half person police department. Unfortunately, from what she'd heard, the new police chief imagined himself Joe Friday, but came across more like Inspector Clouseau or Barney Fife.

Chief Karlman had been recommended for the job by the local state police commander, from whose unit Karlman was retiring. According to Hank Spaight, owner of Registon's only hardware store, member of the town council, and chief town gossip, that should have been the tip-off. 'They couldn't wait to get rid of him over there,' Hank had whispered loudly to Mac during her visit to the hardware store last spring. Karlman had been on the job almost a year at that point, and Hank and a few others had already grown tired of what he described as Karlman's combination of ignorance and arrogance. 'They were forcing early retirement on him, you know. Actually, it's a wonder he made it to retirement, even an early one. Hell, his attic is so vacant, it's a wonder he found his way here from Norwich.'

Mac didn't know if she could embarrass herself in front of this guy. And it would be embarrassing, that's for sure. Are you sure you heard a shot? No. Was it a man or woman who was shot? I don't know. Who did the shooting? Couldn't really see. What kind of boat? Big. Any color description? No. Are you sure of any of this? No.

She decided on a half-way measure during her walk back to the house. She'd call the Registon police office and report hearing a shot on the beach, try to make it a public-safety matter. At least it would be there on the record.

When she got back to the house it was after four, and her mother was already starting to get dressed for the party that night. Riverside University, where both the senior Doctors Griffin taught, was one of the few causes (if not the only) that would stir Elizabeth Mackenzie Griffin into formal wear. E. M. Griffin, Ph.D. was born to wear sensible shoes and tweeds, and that's what she wore nine months out of the year; the other three months she wore mostly navy or lime-green cotton, or linen, or, in her sportier moods, twill. Her mother had no gift for dressing up, as Mac had learned early in life, nor did she care for the kind of occasions that called for it. Despite their loyalty to the university, despite their support of the scholarship fund, if an appearance at tonight's fund-raiser were not *de rigueur*, if it weren't being held right here

10

in Registon at the home of the president of the university, Mac had no doubt that her parents would have sent their regrets.

Mac ran into Stella, their Scottish housekeeper, coming down the stairs with fire in her eye and a long dress draped over her arm. 'The woman's only got two forrrmal gowns,' she said, glaring at Mac. 'I don't see how it can take thrrree hours to make up her mind which she's going to wearrr.' Stella's burr hadn't softened much since her arrival in the United States more than thirty years before. 'And as soon as I get this one prrressed, I'm surrre she'll be switching to the otherrr one.'

Mac decided that prudence dictated that she avoid Stella and her mother for the next hour or so, and she retreated to the kitchen, using the phone there to call the local police. The officer on duty took her report of a gunshot fired, and thanked her for the call.

Once she'd hung up the phone, Mac let the incident at the beach out of her mind. She had to concentrate on pulling herself together to look presentable for the evening, and on getting her parents and her brother out the door on time.

That was no easy feat. Chad didn't walk in from the gallery till close to five, but Mac was able to a) tell him he better hit the showers, fast, or he'd be contending for hot water, and b) warn him to stay out of Stella's way, both by the time he walked through the kitchen.

It took a little longer with her father. Walker Griffin was in the midst of editing his paper, 'Watering the Seeds of Revolution: the Dissolution of the Massachusetts Assembly of 1768 and the Virginian Assembly of 1769,' which was to be included in next spring's *Journal of the American Historical Society,* and he was not happy about being torn away. Mac knew he'd be talking about it all evening, referring to people and incidents of the time as though Peter Jennings had reported them on last night's edition of *ABC World News Tonight.* It was a quirk that Mac, growing up as the child of two historians, had learned to overlook.

Once she got her father sprung from the library, it was time to get herself ready, and she happily unpacked her reliable, wrinkleproof black wool-crepe dress. Simple but elegant, the saleswoman had said, and for once it hadn't been exaggerated sales talk. With plain gold earrings and a gold belt, the dress emphasized Mac's classic blond good looks.

Mac headed down the stairs at six-fifteen and heard Stella wishing her parents a good evening. Fortunately, Stella and her mother had apparently arrived at a working truce and her mother looked quite lovely in her gown; it was not, Mac noticed, the one Stella had been carrying at four o'clock. Her father looked suitably uncomfortable in his tuxedo, but then he never looked comfortable in anything but corduroy and sweaters. Chad came loping down the stairs just as Mac was about to call for him. Punctuality was a thing with her, and tonight's invitation was for six-thirty.

President Hutchinson's house was not quite a mile up River Road from the Griffins'. In a town with some beautiful colonial homes, the Hutchinson house was a standout. The classical proportions of the house were evident as soon as you turned into the tree-lined drive, which opened into a perfect-circle courtyard then closed to a short walkway that led to the center door. The center section of the house was round and domed, and there were rectangular wings to the north and south. The site of the original seventeenth-century Hutchinson home was some fifty yards in back of the current house, closer to the river. The present house was built around the construction that was started in the eighteenth century, which had been added to in the nineteenth, and modernized in the twentieth. And all that time the property had been in the Hutchinson family.

The Hutchinson family had, in fact, been among the first settling families of Registon, and lore had it that it was Christopher Hutchinson who suggested naming the town that in 1648 as a thumb of the nose to Cromwell and his cohorts. This defiance of the Roundheads was a fact that Mac and her siblings had heard repeated reverently and embellished on regularly at various civic and academic gatherings throughout their childhood and adolescence, until it sounded like a gesture equivalent in bravery to that of another local hero, Nathan Hale. One of Mac's fondest memories was of Chad in his skeptical early-adolescent period. At yet another local historical society meeting that their parents had hosted, the chairman faithfully repeated the story yet again. Chad finally blurted out, 'They were three thousand miles away from London, and it took the fastest ship four weeks to get here. How brave could it have been?' In the eyes of the assembled ladies, that remark had branded Chad as a troublemaker who was not properly reverent of Registon's heritage. It branded him a hero in his sisters' eyes.

When Chad turned off River Road into the Hutchinson drive, Mac drew in her breath in a soft whistle. They were pulling out all the stops tonight, she thought, when she saw small torches lining the drive. Chad pulled around to the top of the circle, and Mac and her mother were helped from the car by the parking attendants, obviously students imported from the university for the occasion.

Just inside the front door, the entry hall opened to a large round center hall that was framed with a curving double staircase. It had been a long time since she'd been inside this house, Mac realized – probably not since the last Riverside occasion she'd attended year before last – but she'd always loved this place. She'd always wanted to swoop down that staircase wearing a dress with a train trailing gracefully behind her.

That staircase in fact had been the subject of discussion at yet another historical society meeting in the Griffin home when Mac was in ninth grade. Elizabeth Griffin had chaired a meeting devoted to the architecture of Registon's historic homes. During that meeting it was revealed that the 1840s renovation of the Hutchinson home had yielded a secret room – an *oubliette* as Mac's younger sister Whitney, already entranced with nineteenth-century Gothic fiction, had insisted on calling it, much to the eleven-year-old Chad's disgust – which was located underneath the landing of the double staircase. Mac, caught up in her studies of the Civil War, decided the room *must* have been a hiding place on the Underground Railroad. It took a long conversation with her father before he convinced her that the room had nothing to do with the nineteenth-century Hutchinsons' desire for freedom for runaway slaves, and everything to do with the architect's belated realization that the double-staircase landing could only be supported if it had four walls

14

underneath it. Even looking at the staircase tonight, Mac still liked her version of the story better.

There wasn't any receiving line *per se* – there hadn't been at any Hutchinson gathering since Mrs Hutchinson had passed away five years earlier – but this center hall was where President Hutchinson was greeting the guests. After saying hello to her parents and sending them in the direction of the *hors d'oeuvres*, President Hutchinson turned to Mac and her brother. 'Mackenzie, my dear,' he said, leaning to give her a peck on the cheek, 'it's been too long.'

President Hutchinson was a handsome man, with a head of silver hair that John Forsythe would envy. At the height of the *Dynasty* craze, when Mac was in graduate school in New York, pictures of Forsythe and his co-stars started popping up everywhere. On more than one occasion Mac caught herself wondering, just for an instant, why Avery Hutchinson's picture was on the side of a bus in Manhattan or on the cover of *People* magazine.

He turned now to her brother. 'Chadwick, I was surprised to hear you've taken over Malcolm Howard's gallery. Just heard about it yesterday, as a matter of fact. But delighted, my boy, delighted that it's staying in the hands of a Riverside graduate,' he said as he patted Chad's shoulder. 'And we're always glad when one of our students returns home and makes a contribution to the community.' This last was said with a significant glance toward Mackenzie, letting her know he had still not forgiven her for going to NYU for graduate school, and for compounding that error by staying in New York. In previous conversations, President Hutchinson had also let her know that he held her responsible for the fact that

15

her sister was doing her graduate work in Boston. Only Chad had followed his parents' footsteps, completing both his undergraduate and graduate work at Riverside.

'I understand Malcolm is finally making good on his threat to move to Palm Beach. Where is he, by the way?' Hutchinson continued, apparently not expecting an answer. 'I thought he'd be here by now.' When he glanced past the Griffins to look for Howard, he noticed that there were now other people waiting in the non-receiving line behind them, and he politely moved them along.

Mac and Chad stepped into the garden room where the cocktails and *hors d'oeuvres* were being served, and Chad flagged down one of the student waiters. 'It's amazing how he connects everything back to the school, isn't it? I mean, I'd think the old school ties would start to choke after a while. Can you imagine, Riverside has been his life since he graduated from prep school – what is that – thirty-five, forty years now?'

'Just about the same as Mother and Dad, I guess,' Mac said as she took the first sip of her wine. But while their parents had received both their graduate and undergraduate degrees from Riverside, their ruling passions were their subjects, not necessarily the school.

'Oh God, look who's heading this way,' Chad said with a tone of despair. 'Stephen Franklyn with a "y".'

Mac looked across the room and, sure enough, Stephen Franklyn was zeroing in on them like a precision bomber. She shared Chad's feelings. Franklyn was an uncomfortable man even to look at; his body tended toward pudge, and even his eyeglasses seemed too tight on him, not to mention the strain he was placing on his jacket buttons. He had joined the Riverside faculty when Mac was a senior and Chad a freshman, and Mac knew he was a jerk from the moment she met him eleven years before. She, however, had been spared having him as an instructor. Chad had not.

'Griffin, there you are . . .' he started as he approached and even in those few words his accent was noticeable. Franklyn's mother was British, and he had in fact been born and spent the first ten months of his life in England before his parents' post-war reunion in Rhode Island. Stephen's English accent, however, was now heavier than his mother's and it was Chad who had noticed that Franklyn's accent seemed to get more and more British with each step he took up the academic ladder. He'd been made chairman of the art-history department at Riverside two years before, and now was as hard to understand as some members of the royal family.

'Still going to parties with your big sister, I see,' Franklyn said to Chad, obviously thinking it a witty comment.

Mac noticed Chad inhaling deeply and standing up straighter. 'Want me to beat him up for you, little brother?' she whispered so that only he could hear. Chad smiled despite himself. 'Hello, Franklyn, great to see you as well.'

'So you're giving up a chance at Director of Special Exhibitions at the American Museum, eh, Griffin? All to sell a few more unsuspecting collectors a few more nineteenth-century *landscapes*.' He conveyed a world of contempt in the last word, and Chad had to admit the British accent helped enormously in creating the desired effect.

Chad had to admit, too, that Franklyn's sources were

pretty good. As far as he knew, nobody outside the museum was aware that he'd been offered the Special Exhibitions post. But he didn't want to get into museum politics at the moment, so he decided to take on the sharper of Franklyn's comments. 'I hope to be handling some nineteenth-century work, yes,' Chad replied calmly, 'and I hope to be presenting some new artists as well.'

Franklyn was obviously disappointed at being unable to get a rise from Chad. 'Where's Howard, by the way?' he said, looking over the crowd. 'I hear he's actually talking about moving to Florida.' He made that sound like moving to the dark side of the moon.

Finally deigning to acknowledge her, Franklyn turned to Mac. 'And Mackenzie, I understand you're involved with that singer, Rossellini. I saw your picture at – what was it – the MTV Music Awards?' His accent assisted again in making it sound like they'd been slumming.

'Really, Stephen? I'm only aware of that picture of Peter and me on Page Six of the *Post*, and in the *Daily News*. I didn't take you for a *tabloid* reader.'

Franklyn sputtered in embarrassment, obviously mortified at being caught in a lowbrow indulgence. He pretended to catch the eye of a colleague across the room and excused himself quickly.

Chad wanted to cheer. 'Fabulous, Mac. That was like watching Seles smash one over the net in the old days.'

Mac blew on her knuckles and brushed them across the wool crepe of her dress.

Their parents beckoned them from across the room, and when Mac and Chad joined them her father announced that he wanted them to meet a colleague of his. 'Mackenzie, Chadwick, this is Doctor Timothy Houston, a splendid new addition to our American-history faculty. Tim, my daughter, Doctor Mackenzie Griffin, and my son, Chadwick Griffin.'

Chad stuck his hand out first. 'I decided that there needed to be a patient in the family, along with all these doctors.' It was an old joke, but it usually worked in breaking the ice. It did this time, as well, and Houston smiled agreeably, shaking Chad's hand first, then Mac's.

Houston was a good-looking man in his early thirties, sandy haired and well built, and for a moment Mac wondered if this were going to be an attempt at a fix-up. Then she remembered that it was her parents who were doing the introducing, her parents who didn't pay the slightest bit of attention to mating rituals, and she relaxed.

'Mackenzie, Doctor Houston had an idea about you and Peter . . .' her mother started.

Given that odd opening, Mac was no longer relaxed. What kind of idea did he have about her and Peter? When she looked at Houston and saw him giving her a rather detailed look-over, her antennae perked up to full alert. She'd noticed over the last few months, ever since her name had been linked with Peter Rossellini's, a phenomenon she'd started describing as 'celebrity envy'. Upon learning she was involved with a well known pop star, certain men would come on to her outrageously. It was as though they believed that if they won her over, they'd somehow be one up on a famous guy. Another example of what too much – or too little – testosterone could occasionally do to some people.

'Actually, it's more about Mr Rossellini than you, I'm afraid,' Houston said.

Well, if this was a come-on, it was a different one, Mac thought, feeling slightly put down. Maybe it wasn't celebrity envy after all.

'I'm faculty coordinator for the silent auction, you see. And I was wondering if we could add to tonight's auction something – a dinner perhaps, or a concert – with you and Mr Rossellini.'

So relax, Mackenzie, she said to herself. This guy's not after you, he's after money. 'That would be a wonderful idea, Dr Houston, but I wouldn't feel comfortable committing Peter to something like that without checking with him first, and I'm afraid he's in Japan at the moment.'

Houston didn't bother to hide his disappointment.

'How about if I promise to put in outlandish bids on a couple of things tonight?' Mac said. 'Would that help?'

'Maybe,' Houston said, letting her off the hook gracefully.

Mac and Chad joined the informal queue of people edging their way around the perimeter of the room, reading the enticing descriptions of the items being offered in the silent auction. Riverside had one of these events every other year, and tonight's offerings were of the usual high standards. The fund-raisers had decided that a silent auction was the most tasteful way to raise money that anybody could think of, and it was twice or three times as effective with the little twist that President Hutchinson had put on it. Bids were made in the form of checks, and, of course, whoever wrote the check for the highest amount actually received the prize. Those putting in losing bids had to specify on their checks if they wanted the check returned or if it was a contribution to the scholarship fund. After the first year, when President Hutchinson publicly returned a few checks to people, all the bidding checks had been contributions, and the scholarship fund grew by two and a half times the amount they'd estimated.

It was hard to judge what a winning bid would be on this night's offerings. The descriptions, done in perfect calligraphy, were posted next to an old photo or a pen-and-ink illustration that captured the essence of the item being offered, and the selection of the photographs and illustrations indicated a real wit on the part of whoever coordinated it all.

The offerings included a case of wine (illustrated by a 1930s advertisement for a hangover remedy), a weekend in Boston, a ride in a hot-air balloon (illustrated with a mini-poster from *The Wizard of Oz),* a weekend cruise on the Connecticut River in President Hutchinson's own boat, ski weekends in Vermont (pictured as a leg in traction), rare books, weekend getaways in the Caribbean, and antique maps. All were brilliantly described and had minimum bids indicated; the minimums showed that the organizers weren't kidding around about raising funds. She'd have to find out if it was Dr Houston who arranged this presentation, Mac decided, and congratulate him if he did.

Within a few minutes the guests were discreetly shooed into the ballroom, where fifteen round tables for eight had been set up, along with a rectangular table for ten at the front. The room looked absolutely beautiful. The tables each had centerpieces that captured the late fall colors with chrysanthemums, waxed leaves, and pine cones. The candles were a different color on each table, and the candles and the sconce lamps at regular intervals along the wall were the main source of light in the room. Mac and her brother followed their parents to their table, where, they were dismayed to learn, Stephen Franklyn was also seated. On the brighter side, Dr Houston joined them as well. Rounding out the table was a couple in their early forties, Dr and Mrs DeVargas; Dr DeVargas was a colleague of their mother's in the classics department.

The sound of the room soon diminished to the soft hum of many separate conversations going on simultaneously. It wasn't until the main-course plates were being cleared that President Hutchinson rose to speak.

'Ladies and gentlemen, if I may have your attention just briefly,' Hutchinson said into the pencil-slim microphone next to the almost-invisible plexiglas podium. The sound of his voice fitted the room perfectly, as Mac knew it would. There had been an 'episode' a few years ago, when a student from the communications department who had been in charge of setting up the loudspeaker system for one of the events at the Hutchinson home had gotten distracted by a pretty young woman working for the caterer. The wires had been crossed, and the volume hadn't been checked, so when President Hutchinson went to the microphone that evening, the high-volume feedback had practically destroyed the hearing of all the assembled guests, not to mention anyone within a thousand yards of the Hutchinson home. President Hutchinson's wrath in response to that lapse had become legendary, and the head of the a/v team now made it his

22

personal responsibility to check out the very high-end microphone and amplification system they had purchased for the president's use.

'I'll begin by introducing one of our distinguished guests. Those of you familiar with Riverside's history will know this story, but I'm afraid you'll just have to listen to it again.' A brief swell of polite laughter traveled the room.

'What do you think? Is it going to be the "boys at Harvard" speech?' Chad said softly to Mac.

'Probably.'

Hutchinson continued. 'Riverside was founded in 1638, but as much as we'd like to give those boys at Harvard a run for their money in claiming to be the country's oldest university, we can't. Riverside was founded as a school for boys – what we'd call a prep school today – and it remained that until the 1820s. It expanded its curriculum and its mission, and by 1868 was chartered by the state of Connecticut as a full degree-granting university of the liberal arts. I'm sure many of you remember the splendid 125th anniversary celebration we had not long ago, following as it did by only five years the splendid 350th anniversary celebration. We've learned that an institution can never have too many anniversaries to celebrate.' He reached for his water glass to let his humor sink in. 'But I digress. The fact that Riverside came into existence in 1638 was due to the beneficence of one man – Lord Boleigh, who donated the land the original school occupied and on which our main administration building still sits – and who endowed the school for its first thirty years. That splendid tradition of generosity continues in this the – twelfth, is it? – generation since the founding Lord Boleigh, and I am pleased to present to you one of Riverside's most beloved benefactors, Lord Boleigh.'

The man who had been sitting to President Hutchinson's right rose and waved at the audience with that peculiar wave that seems to be exclusive to English nobility and Italian popes: an almost balletic arching of the hand, cupping it toward oneself, and then wagging it a little.

Lord Boleigh was in his fifties now – a pleasant-enough-looking man of less than average height, whose broad, squat face was one of the few Mac had ever seen that cried out for some distinguishing characteristic. A mustache, perhaps. Even muttonchops would help. Given the fact that Boleigh was pronounced 'bully', though, there was some danger. In the hands of the wrong barber he could turn into a parody of his name, and even more of a caricature of the archetypal privileged Englishman that he already was.

'This guy is unbelievable,' Chad said, a little louder than his previous comment, so that he could be heard over the smattering of applause that greeted Lord Boleigh's wave. 'He shows up at more Riverside events than my class alumni chairman.'

'Reliving the glory days of his family, don't you know,' Stephen Franklyn said. 'That is if any of those west-country families had any glory days.' He reached for his wine glass, as he'd been doing frequently through the meal. One of the waiters showed up to replenish it as soon as he put it down.

Lord Boleigh had taken his seat again, and President Hutchinson turned back to his dinner guests, microphone in hand. 'Before we announce the results of tonight's silent auction, I do want to thank each and every one of you for your support of Riverside and of its mission.'

'Uh-oh,' Chad whispered. 'It's The Speech.' The word 'mission' was always the tip-off

'Short or long version?' Mac whispered back.

'He looks pretty wound up to me. I'll take the long version.'

'Okay, I've got the short. For the usual quarter?'

'Let's make it a dollar. Neither one of us has any change.'

'Are you two betting on President Hutchinson's speech again?' asked their mother. Mac and Chad smiled like guilty twelve-year-olds, and their mother turned back to face the head table with a 'tsk' and the shake of the head that was the universal gesture of mothers.

Hutchinson was just getting going, having explained that the word 'mission' was not inappropriately used. 'It is our obligation, and indeed our privilege, to bring to our students the magnificent panorama of Western civilization. From the Academy of ancient Greece to the proud civic heritage of the Roman empire, from the misnamed Dark Ages, when the civilizing force that became known as Christianity was quietly taking root across Europe and which brought us, on the cusp of the Renaissance, the glories of the Gothic cathedral. The Renaissance itself, that inspired re-awakening, that fostered the curiosity that led to the Age of Exploration, which has a very personal meaning for those of us fortunate enough to be part of the glorious American experiment. And without the American experiment, would the Age of Enlightenment have shone as brightly? Would the Industrial Revolution been as revolutionary? And would the Technological Revolution have even been possible?'

Hutchinson was building to a full head of steam when he stopped himself. 'Those of you who know me know I'm quite passionate on the subject, but I think it's time to announce the winners of tonight's auction. So I'll ask Dr Houston, who's done such a marvelous job organizing the event, to come to the microphone.'

As Houston headed to the front of the room, Mac leaned toward her brother. 'Short version. You owe me a buck.'

'Who'd have believed it? I thought we were set for a good ten minutes,' Chad replied.

Stephen Franklyn suddenly spoke, to the entire table and to no one in particular. 'Hutchinson's deluding himself if he thinks we're presenting the history of Western civilization to our students anymore. I can't even get students to look at medieval art, because it looks *funny* to them. One girl actually had the audacity to ask me why the twentieth-century course had to focus so much on Picasso. His abstracts are so *ugly*, she said.' Franklyn took a large gulp of his wine, and it looked like he was warming to his subject. 'Well, what can you expect of a generation who've been told that LeRoy Neimann and Crisco – or whatever the hell his name is – are artists.'

He was getting louder, and Chad and Mac did a quick eyeball consultation. Chad leaned toward Franklyn. 'Stephen, why don't we head to the rest room, splash a little cold water on the face?'

Franklyn hadn't even heard him, and was obviously unaware that the others at the table had become uncomfortable. He set his glass down with a thump and started in again, obviously eager to share this next point. 'I had one student – a girl of eighteen or nineteen – tell me that I was wrong to refer to Titian as the greatest colorist of the sixteenth century. She thought his colors were garish. Well, I said, on my side I have thirty years of training and study and approximately four hundred years of art scholarship. On your side, however, we have your *opinion*. Not to be dismissed, certainly, coming as it does from the runner-up for Miss Massachusetts.' He glanced around the table triumphantly. 'She actually was, too. Runner-up for Miss Massachusetts in that Miss America beauty pageant.' He paused dramatically and put a hand to his mouth in a pantomime of false distress. 'Excuse me, scholarship program. But the only place your opinion is equal to mine, Miss Runner-Up for Miss Massachusetts, is at the ballot box! And I have questions about that!'

'Stephen's definitely been over-served,' Chad whispered to Mac, using one of their favorite euphemisms from their parents' vocabulary. He looked up to see his father signaling him, and the two Griffin gentlemen coordinated their approach – one from the right, one from his left – to escort Stephen Franklyn to the rest room. He got in his last licks, however. 'It all started with opening up the museums, you know,' he said to those still seated. 'This unwashed rabble lines the halls and you can't even hear yourself think anymore.' Chad pulled back his chair, but Franklyn was oblivious. 'Have you been to the Metropolitan in New York? Or the Athenaeum? And they don't even know what they're looking at!' He was still talking as they got him out the archway into the hall.

'I hate to say this of a colleague, but what a thoroughly

unpleasant man!' Dr Griffin said, and Mackenzie stared almost open-mouthed. For her mother, that was very strong language indeed.

By the time Chad and her father returned, Dr Houston was just finishing up the announcement of the auction winners. Chad was the owner of a case of a premium wine from a new Connecticut vineyard, and her parents were the winners of the weekend trip on President Hutchinson's boat, but Mac had lost out on the rare books. Apparently her check wasn't big enough to win, just big enough to be a . . . contribution. She tried to smile graciously.

It turned out to be a fairly early evening, and they were able to leave by 10:15. Mac was grateful, since, over the course of the evening, she'd felt a stiffness coming on from their unpacking and moving efforts of the last two days.

She was grateful again that they'd made an early night of it when she woke up the next morning. She'd slept well, the stiffness was gone, and she was debating about taking another walk on the beach. She would wait until after her first cup of coffee, however, before she made that decision, and she was standing in the kitchen waiting for the coffee maker to finish dripping when the phone rang. She glanced at the clock; it was only seven-thirty. A call so early on a Sunday morning was a surprise.

'Miss Griffin, please,' said the voice on the other end of the line. Mac didn't bother to correct him. It was confusing enough that both her parents were Doctor Griffin, and that her younger sister soon would be. Around Registon, she was still called Miss Griffin.

'Yes, this is she.'

'Chief Karlman, Registon police, ma'am.'

'Yes.'

'I understand you reported hearing a gunshot down at the beach yesterday afternoon.'

'That's right.'

'Can you tell me about what time that was, ma'am?'

'The time that I heard the shot was between three-fifteen and three-thirty. I'm sorry I can't be more precise than that.'

'That's just fine, ma'am. That's a big help for now. One more thing, would you be able to tell me where you were on the beach when you heard the shot?'

'Yes, I think I could show you.'

'If I sent a car around for you in the next few minutes, ma'am, do you think you could come down to the beach now?'

'I'd be happy to help, Chief, if you'll tell me what's going on.'

'We had a body wash up on the beach here, Miss Griffin. Somebody spotted it just after dawn.'

Mac's stomach sank. Maybe she had witnessed a murder, after all. 'Yes, Chief. Send the car over, and I'll be ready.' And there are a few other things I can tell you, too, she thought.

'Thank you, ma'am, Officer Henson will be there inside five minutes.' He was about to hang up.

'Chief . . . ?'

'Yes ma'am?'

Mac took a deep breath. 'Do you know who . . . ?' It was hard to finish the sentence, just like it was always hard to speak of the recently dead.

'We have a tentative identification, ma'am. Malcolm Howard. Lived right here in Registon. You probably knew him.'

Not well, at least not as well as Chad and her parents did. She'd have to tell them as soon as they woke up. Well, she thought, her mind heading off on a different track, that answered the question of why Malcolm Howard hadn't made it to the fund-raiser last night.

Mac knew the answer to the next question before she asked it. She knew that the police wouldn't be calling her unless her phone call of the day before had some bearing on their investigation. 'Chief, Mr Howard had been shot, hadn't he?'

'Yes, ma'am,' the Chief said with a tired certainty. 'In the head. At close range. He took a bullet right in the brain.'

TWO

Whoever had told Mac that Chief Karlman fancied himself Joe Friday had gotten the wrong television program. He wasn't the Jack Webb type at all. However, Mac would have bet real money that he'd spent entirely too much time in his younger years watching *Hawaii Five-0*.

Karlman had been officiating at the scene since Mac arrived; he'd asked if she could take a look at the body since he didn't have a confirmed i.d. yet. Not that hers would be, of course, he just wanted to make sure they're talking about the right guy. Mac knew what he really wanted to see is if she got squeamish looking at a corpse.

Her first glimpse of Malcolm Howard's body had been a surprise; she'd forgotten how much damage water could do to a body even in just twelve to fifteen hours. He was bloated, and his skin had that strange color that immersion in water brings, but his face was unmarked. When Mac moved closer to the body, however, she saw that the back quarter of his skull was virtually gone.

While Mac recounted what she'd seen and heard yesterday afternoon, she kept an eye out on the road, since she expected Chad to join them any minute. She'd gone to his room as soon as she'd hung up the phone, and while she wasn't positive if she'd gotten the details through to him, she was pretty sure he knew to come to the stretch of beach east of the old jetty. Just as she was finishing, she heard the sound of a motor. Mac looked up to the dirt road that led to the beach from Old Shore Road. Chad was heading toward them.

'Mac,' he said as soon as he drew close enough to be heard, 'did you say to me what I think you said to me? Malcolm Howard's been shot?'

Mac nodded. She, Chief Karlman and the other officer were blocking Chad's view of Howard's body. 'He's dead, Chad.'

'You're her brother – Chadwick Griffin?' Karlman said. Chad nodded.

'Your sister tells me you knew Malcolm Howard pretty well.'

'I wasn't a close personal friend or anything like that. But I've known him for years, and I just bought the River's End Gallery from him. This past week.'

'We haven't been able to track down any family as yet—' Karlman started again.

'His mother died about six weeks ago, and that was the last family he had,' Chad interrupted. 'He had a sister, but she died several years ago, I believe.'

'Married?' asked Karlman.

'Divorced,' answered Chad. 'For a long time, I think. What would you say, Mac? Fifteen years?'

'That would be about right,' Mac said. 'He moved back here and started the gallery the year I was graduating prep school, and I think Mother and Dad said he came back right after his divorce.'

This didn't appear to be a fruitful area for Karlman. He moved on. 'You'd be able to identify him for us?' he said to Chad.

Chad was surprised. 'Yes, I think so.'

Karlman and the officer stepped aside, giving Chad a clear view of the upper half of Howard's body. Mac could tell that the image hit him like a lightning bolt. 'Oh, jeez,' he said, paling. Mac stepped to his side. He looked at her, then back at the body, and finally to Karlman. 'Yes, that's Malcolm Howard.'

'Maybe you can answer a few questions for us—' Karlman started.

'In a minute, Chief,' Mac said. 'Give him a minute.' She walked Chad over to one of the huge boulders that lined this section of the beach and Chad sat down. Mackenzie stood in front of him, her back to the police officers, deliberately blocking their view. 'You okay?'

'My stomach is still deciding which end is up. Honest to God, Mackenzie – that was gross! I know you've been around this kind of thing before, but do you ever get used to it? Does it ever stop bothering you?'

'When it stops bothering you, then you're in trouble.'

She moved next to him, hitched herself up onto the boulder and they sat quietly for a few minutes. Then Mac asked, 'Feeling better?'

'Sort of. I'm trying to decide if I'm better off or worse off that I didn't have any coffee.'

'Probably better. But we're gonna need some soon.' She

hopped down from the boulder. 'This shouldn't take too long. Ready to answer some of his questions?'

'Yeah. Let's go.'

They walked up to Karlman, who was busy talking to Officer Henson. He turned his attention to them as they approached. 'Wish we could figure out what the hell's going on here. Henson just got a call from the unit that we sent to Howard's home. He lived in one of the carriage houses on the north end of town, you know. Seems like the place was almost all packed up.'

'That makes sense,' Chad said. 'He was moving to Florida. I can't remember when he said he was leaving exactly, but I know it was soon.'

'Well, somebody tried to unpack him. The whole place had been tossed pretty good. Boxes ripped open, stuff all over the floor. Apparently it's going to be a nightmare to lift any prints that were left behind.' He finished with a weary shake of his head. Then he looked back at Chad. 'So what can you tell me?'

'Not much, I'm afraid. I've known Howard for years, but it's not like we were really friends. When I was here visiting my parents in late August I ran into him and, almost as a joke, I said if he was ever interested in selling the gallery to let me know. I got a call from him down in Washington about a month later that he was interested. I realized later that he called me the day after his mother died.'

'So, in buying this gallery from him, you see him much in the last couple of months?' Karlman asked.

'No, once we agreed on basic terms, most of the contact was through our lawyers.' Chad paused, and his forehead wrinkled as a new thought occurred. 'I did think it was odd that Malcolm insisted on the deal being absolutely confidential until it was closed. It wasn't until the day before the closing, when I came up to do the walk-through of the gallery with him, and go through some of the paperwork, that he finally agreed to the wording of the announcement of the sale.'

'Why do you think he was so secretive?' Karlman asked.

'I have no idea. Like I said, I've known the man for years, but I didn't know him well. He did seem a little twitchy at the closing, but I figured that was because he had so much on his mind; closing up shop here, moving his home – that's a lot to handle at once.'

From the expression on his face, you could tell that Karlman wasn't convinced people got that nervous about moving. 'Can you think of any enemies he might have had?'

Chad glanced quickly at Mac, then back at the Chief, surprised at the question. 'No,' he said. 'What kind of enemies would an art dealer in a small town like this have?'

'Maybe some irate artist who decided Howard was taking too big a cut?' Karlman suggested with a too-knowing tilt to his head.

'I don't think so, Chief,' Chad replied, suppressing a smile at how off-the-mark Karlman's assessment was. 'Almost all of the artists Howard dealt in are dead, and I've seen the books he kept on the living ones. He wasn't cheating anybody.'

'We'll see about that,' Karlman said with a somewhat patronizing tone. 'We'll see about that.'

* * *

Chief Karlman kept them for another fifteen minutes, so it was after nine by the time Mac and Chad got back to their parents' house. They sat at the trestle table in the kitchen, both of them having decided, after the scene at the beach, that 'just coffee' would be sufficient for breakfast.

Their parents were shocked to learn about Malcolm Howard's death, and Mac's father went to the phone immediately to call President Hutchinson. He returned a few minutes later, the expression on his face even sadder than when he left. 'Hutchinson says, unless there are other directions in any will they find, he'll probably have to make the funeral arrangements, since Howard had no family left. I hadn't thought of that before. Sad.' None of them at the table – Mac, Chad, or their mother – said anything. They just sat together in the silence.

Around eleven-thirty, Chad announced that he was heading over to the gallery to take care of a few things. Mac asked if he needed any help, but he declined her offer. Besides, it was Sunday, and that meant one of Stella's big dinners, and that meant Mac would be on kitchen duty early afternoon.

Stella's Sunday dinners were always big, always delicious, and always served at 2:30 on the dot. Knowing how sacrosanct Stella's schedule was, and knowing that Chad had said he was only going to be an hour or so, Mac began to notice the time around 1:15. At 1:30, the phone rang. Stella answered, and after a hearty 'Wherrre are ya, lad?' and an answer that evidently didn't satisfy her, she said 'She's right here,' and handed the phone to Mackenzie. 'It's your brrrother,' she said. 'Remind him the roast comes out of the oven in thirty minutes.'

Chad's voice sounded funny from the first syllable. 'Mac, I know this sounds like the old game, but don't say anything, okay?'

'Okay,' she responded hesitantly.

'I need you to get over here right now.'

'What . . . ?'

'Don't say anything.' He sounded worse to her ears. 'Just get over here.'

'At the gallery?' she asked, trying to sound cheery for Stella's benefit.

'Yeah.'

'Are you . . .'

He cut in on her again. 'Mac, just get here.' Mac heard the phone clunk down in her ear.

'Okay,' Mac said, still cheery, pretending she was still talking to her brother. She knew that getting past Stella was going to take a little finessing. Even as she, a trained professional in psychology, contemplated how she was going to lie to Stella, it amazed her how the authority figures from childhood could retain their power.

'I'm just going over to the gallery to help Chad with something for a minute,' she said, avoiding eye contact.

'Did you tell the boy the roast will be out of the oven in thirty minutes?' Stella asked, knowing full well that Mackenzie hadn't.

'I'll tell him. I'm going to go pick him up.'

'He took his car, didn't he?' Stella asked, her eyebrow raised.

'Yeah,' Mac said, 'but . . . he needs help . . . moving something.' She groaned inwardly, knowing that she sounded like a fourteen-year-old. She reached for her purse and car keys, both of which were always kept by the kitchen door. 'Be back in a flash.'

It was a two-minute drive to the gallery, if that, but it seemed much longer to Mac. What in the world was the matter with Chad? He sounded awful on the phone.

She pulled up in front of the gallery and quickly walked to the front door.

In this prosperous town of expensive cars, there was no reason for her to notice the expensive dark sedan parked beyond the gallery, on the other side of the street.

After Chad had replaced the phone in its cradle, it took almost every bit of his remaining strength to walk to the door and unlock it for her. Then he realized that it wasn't locked. Of course, the bozos had hardly locked it behind them when they left. He managed to make it to the one straight-backed side chair they'd left in the front gallery and slumped into it.

He tried to get it straight in his mind what had happened. He knew Mackenzie would want a complete report.

He glanced at his watch. According to the digital readout it was 1:33. Damn! He'd been crumpled there on the floor for almost forty minutes.

He'd gotten to the gallery just before noon, like he'd planned. He wanted to continue going through the files he'd started reviewing yesterday afternoon.

After an hour – he'd looked at his watch, and it was just 12:45 – he was wrapping up what he'd wanted to accomplish. He'd heard what sounded like footsteps in the front room and started to head toward the front, thinking it was probably Mac, coming to nudge him home.

But as he stepped into the middle gallery he saw two well-dressed men – both in good-looking suits, neither wearing a raincoat or overcoat, even though the temperature was still in the low 40s. They were both big men, as well, easily a few inches over six feet. Each man had an arm up to his head, in a gesture like they were going to remove their hats. But then he realized that neither wore a hat. What both of them were doing was adjusting a mask. That was Chad's big tip-off that these weren't art patrons inquiring about the future of the gallery. They both had on masks. And Halloween had been last Thursday night.

The two men walked toward him and met him at the rear of the center gallery. The one on the right, the bigger of the two, grabbed Chad by the front of his shirt and asked, 'Okay, where is it?'

'Where's what?' Chad asked, still hoping in a secret compartment that it was some weird Halloween thing and it would all be cleared up if he answered a question correctly. Sort of like Jeopardy. Except on Jeopardy, of course, you have to question the answers.

'Don't get cute with me, where is it?'

Cute was the last thing on Chad's mind. Chad rarely thought of himself as a tall man, but he never thought of himself as short – a luxury that someone who is six foot one can usually afford. So when this very large, very strong man pulled him up and held him so that his feet weren't entirely planted on the floor, the sensation was quite creepy.

'Come on, sonny boy, where is it?' the man said again, leaning his masked face toward Chad's. The rubber of the mask distorted his voice, giving it a slight echo. And there was an odd smell about the man, too, that probably came from the mask as well.

'Where's *what*? I don't know what the hell you're talking about!'

The other man, still standing further into the room, finally chimed in. 'Maybe he needs a little help in remembering. Why don't you hold him?'

With that, the bigger guy pulled Chad around, grabbed hold of his upper arms, and pinned them across his back. He turned him into position and held him while the other gut-punched him.

After the second jab to his stomach, the guy hit Chad with an uppercut to the jaw that had him seeing stars, then another uppercut. Chad felt blood around his mouth, but he wasn't sure if it was coming from his lip or nose or where.

'Is your memory improving now, asshole?' the hitter asked.

'Believe me, I don't know what you're talking about.' His own voice sounded strange to him, like he wasn't pronouncing the words well.

There was a hesitation, a body language from the hitter that looked like he was really listening to Chad, like he was believing him. Then he gut-punched him again for good measure and said to the other one, 'Leave it. I don't think he knows shit.'

With that, the first guy released Chad's arms and he crumpled to the floor. He heard their shoes clicking across the hardwood floor as they walked out through the front gallery, and out the front door. He heard the sound of them pulling their masks off before they closed the door.

He'd looked at his watch then. It was 12:54. By the time he cleared his head and determined that he could move, he realized how very much it hurt to move. He inched his way back through the center gallery, pulling himself across the floor. After an enormous effort, he finally reached the phone in the rear office and called Mac.

Mackenzie found him, sitting on the lone chair in the front gallery to the left of the front door, over in the shadow.

'Chad! Oh, shit! What happened to you?' Mackenzie cried out when she saw him. The usually dapper Chad had his shirt-tails hanging out, blood was streaking down from the side of his mouth and dripping from his chin, and he had a puffy bruise on one cheekbone and the beginnings of a real shiner over the other eye.

He'd been beaten. Badly beaten.

Strangely, that's when Chad started to get nervous. He knew he must look pretty bad if his sister had resorted to profanity. Everybody knew that Mackenzie considered swearing a symptom of a weak vocabulary.

Sitting in the dark sedan that was parked about fifty feet beyond the gallery on the opposite side of King Street, Sonny unconsciously drummed his fingers on the top of the wheel. It was a pretty controlled movement, given how pissed he was. The Patriots were playing Buffalo this afternoon. It was a big game in the first winning season the Pats had had in he couldn't remember how long, but here he was parked in the middle of this not even one-horse town in Connecticut. Hell, the place only had one stoplight from what he'd seen on the drive in.

He checked his watched for the fifth or sixth time since they'd gotten back in the car. They'd been sitting here for forty-five minutes already, and instead of the guy coming out, some woman had gone in. The sister, probably, if the information they had was correct.

Sonny had figured out yesterday after they'd searched the house and come up zippo that they'd have to be back here today. If they'd come earlier like he wanted to, maybe they coulda gotten in and out before noon. But no. Buster needed his beauty sleep this morning.

He looked over at Buster, snoozing in the passenger seat. Jesus, this guy could piss him off even when he was asleep. It had been – what? three months? – no, just since Labor Day that they'd been working together and the kind of hate Sonny felt for Buster had the tang of a hate three, four years old.

Ever since he'd arrived Buster had been lording it over Sonny with comments like 'That's not the way we did it in Boston' or cracks like 'Let me show you how it's *really* done' or 'Jesus, if that's how you do it, no wonder you've always been stuck in Rhode Island.' Crap like that went right up his nose.

Like Rhode Island was in some armpit of the world instead of forty-five minutes from Boston. And like this asshole wasn't stuck in Rhode Island with him. Buster had been sent down by the old man's associates in Boston because he fucked up something in a big way. Sonny hadn't been able to nail down all the details yet, but he'd gotten dribs and drabs. It wasn't like Buster was stealing money from the associates or anything, 'cause then he'd just be dead. And it wasn't like he was screwin' one of the bosses' daughters or anything like that either, 'cause then he'd be dead with his balls cut off. No, Buster's exile from Beantown had something to do with him fucking up a job. And given the way things were going, Rhode Island was goin' to be looking pretty good to ol' Buster soon, once they shipped him off to – where? Maybe Albany or someplace. Because he'd been fuckin' up here pretty consistently since he arrived, too. First it was getting the old man lost twice when he was driving him back in September, which is how Sonny ended up doin' all the driving these days. And then when he didn't pay attention to the old man's orders last week. Jesus, Sonny thought the old guy was gonna have a stroke right in front of his eyes. He'd never heard the old man yell at *anybody* like that, with the veins poppin' out on his forehead and everything. Buster stood there and took it, Sonny had to give him credit for that. Although he did have a weird look in his eye, like he was listening but not really hearing.

Maybe that's what happened up in Boston, Sonny thought. Maybe Buster's weirdness got the best of him one day. Because he was weird, that was for sure. He had one of those mean crazy tempers, and sometimes he really seemed to be almost gettin' off when he was whackin' on somebody. Sonny enjoyed a good fight as much as the next guy, but it was creepy the way Buster enjoyed it. The gleam in his eye wasn't a normal good-fight gleam. It was a sick-in-the-head gleam.

Like today with the masks. Sonny figured if ski masks were good enough for his uncle and his cousin and his brother before him, they were good enough for him. But no, Buster had made a thing about buying these damn Halloween masks. Sonny could still smell the funny rubber smell on his skin and his hands. At least it distracted from Buster's goddamn cologne which he'd poured on this morning as usual.

He looked at his watch again. It must be the end of the first quarter, beginning of the second. He didn't even dare turn on the radio, because then he'd have to listen to Buster talk about all the times he'd seen the Patriots in person at the stadium, about how good the beer was at the stadium, how much better the hot dogs were than anyplace in godforsaken Rhode Island or Connecticut, and how could people live in these two-bit towns, anyway? And then Sonny would have to punch Buster out and the old man wouldn't like that.

Shit. A cop pulled up across the street. Sonny wasn't worried that they'd be spotted, since the windows had a deep tint. And this guy didn't seem to be looking around before he headed into the gallery, anyway. Shit on a brick this time. Here they'd been waiting for close to an hour for the Griffin kid to leave so they could search the gallery. But now that the cops were here they weren't going to get into this place today – or anytime soon.

He turned the ignition key and flipped on the radio as he pulled away from the kerb. Buster woke up instantly with a 'Wha's goin'on?' Sonny didn't care if he was awake now. He wouldn't have to listen to Buster's bullshit once they hit I-95, and maybe he'd be able to catch the second half.

Stella's Sunday dinner was postponed, for the first time on record, till 3:30. After hearing Chad's story, Mac had called the police. When the dispatcher seemed reluctant to send an officer, Mac insisted that he contact Chief Karlman. 'This may be part of an on-going murder investigation, officer,' she warned. She was assured that a car would be dispatched.

Karlman himself showed up a few minutes later. He'd been back at Howard's home, going through Malcolm Howard's papers.

'Some shiner you're gonna have there, Griffin,' he said as soon as he saw Chad's face. 'Now, Miss Griffin,' he said, turning to Mac, 'what makes you think this is connected to Malcolm Howard's death?'

'Simple. Chad buys this gallery from Malcolm Howard. Two days later, Malcolm Howard turns up dead. The next day, two men in masks walk into said gallery, demanding a mysterious "it" and beat up Chad when he can't accommodate them.'

'Could be, could be,' Karlman said, his bottom lip jutting out as he slipped into his pensive mode. 'Refresh my memory,' he said, turning to Chad. 'Did they ever mention Howard's name?'

'No,' Chad said, talking over the damp cloth he held to his mouth.

'They ever say "it" was an art thing, or was it just "it"?'

'No,' Chad replied, stressing Karlman's terminology, 'they never said "it" was an art thing.'

'So we don't know for sure that these guys are tied to Howard.'

'Chief—' Mac started, annoyed.

'For all we know, these guys could have followed you up from Washington—'

'What?!' Chad cried out, a little too vigorously for the state of his mouth.

'But what we'll do,' Karlman said, trying to placate, 'we'll keep an eye on the place. And you give us a call if anything else happens.'

Mac watched as he walked out the door and down the walkway. During her contact with the Chief in the last several hours she had formed an opinion about him, one that differed slightly from the conventional wisdom. It wasn't so much that Karlman was out-and-out dumb, although he wasn't any too bright. It was more that he was lazy, especially about things that didn't interest him. Given the energy he'd displayed this morning, a murder on the beach held some interest for him. A mugging inside a gallery apparently did not. Mac turned back to Chad. 'I normally have the highest respect for the police officers I come into contact with. I think I'll have to make an exception for Chief Karlman.'

By the time Mac got her brother home – in her car – it was close to three. The story that 'Chad had hurt himself slightly' held up only until they made it into the kitchen and Stella got a look at his face. Her cry of outrage brought their parents running.

'Who did this to ya, lad?' she said, sounding like she was going to go hunt them down.

Mackenzie and Chad gave them the abridged version of the attack, and confirmed that the police had been called. They left out the details of Karlman's departure.

After a few ice-packs and a clean shirt for Chad, they all

moved toward the dining room for dinner. 'Malcolm Howard shot on the beach,' Elizabeth Griffin said with a frown. 'Men beating Chadwick up right on King Street. What in the world is going on?'

THREE

Mackenzie's classes didn't resume until Wednesday, so she wasn't planning on heading back to the city until mid-day Tuesday. Her parents did have classes Monday, however, and they were out of the house by eight o'clock.

Mac took advantage of the leisurely early morning hours; she dallied over the newspaper a little longer than usual and indulged in the luxury of a weekday walk on the beach. When she got back, Stella had a fresh pot of coffee brewing.

'Have you heard Chad up and around yet?' she asked Stella.

'Up and around and gone,' she was told.

'Gone? Where'd he go?'

'Said he was going to the pharmacy and the post office. He'll be back shortly.'

Shortly it was. Chad appeared at the kitchen door within ten minutes, his eyes alight with a certain look Mac remembered well from childhood. She recognized it even through the bruise that was blossoming over his cheekbone.

'Stel, you're a princess,' Chad said, reaching around her with his one free hand to grab one of the sweet rolls she'd carefully placed on a plate mid-counter. 'Mac, grab a mug of coffee for me would you, and then come here. I've got something to show you.'

Mac obligingly poured him a mug of coffee and, carrying her own cup, backed her way through the swinging door that led to the dining room. 'Why aren't we sitting in the kitchen?' she asked.

'Shh,' Chad said, eyeing the door to make sure Stella was still on the other side of it. 'Wait 'til I show you this.'

Mac set down the mugs on the table, which still wore the padded tablecloth from yesterday's dinner. Chad was spreading out some envelopes and paper.

'What's all this stuff?'

'I had to go down to the pharmacy this morning. We ran out of whatever that stuff was that Stella was putting on my cut. While I was there, I stopped at the post office to check the box.'

'You don't have a post-office box,' Mac replied, sipping her coffee.

'I do now. Or should I say, River's End Gallery has one. Malcolm Howard gave me the key last week just before the closing. We'd decided that I might as well keep it. Wouldn't have to change address for utilities, other stuff for the gallery, that kind of thing.'

'And . . . ?'

'So I went and checked the box this morning, and look what I got.' He shoved an envelope across the table to her.

Mac looked down. It was a standard business envelope, bulging in the center a bit. It was hand addressed to 'Chadwick Griffin, River's End Gallery, PO Box 309, Registon, Conn.'

'It's addressed to you,' Mac said. 'Isn't it a little early for you to be getting mail already?'

'Look at the return address,' Chad said.

She did. It read 'Howard, Turner's Road, Registon.' 'It's from Malcolm Howard?' She looked over at Chad and he nodded.

'Open it,' he said.

Mac pulled out the single piece of paper that held an oddly-shaped key. The key had a standard-length shank to it, but the head was quite thick and covered with a hard blue plastic which had a number embossed on it, The number was A-34. Mac picked up the key in one hand and unfolded the piece of paper with her other. In large capital letters, the writer – presumably Malcolm Howard – had scrawled HE MUST BE STOPPED.

' "He must be stopped"!? Yo.' She looked up and caught Chad's eye. 'What do you think this means?'

'I have no idea, but from the postmark on there' – Mac quickly turned the envelope over again, and saw that it had been hand-canceled, presumably because of the bulk of the key, on Saturday – 'Malcolm Howard sent that to me a few hours before he was killed.'

'What are you going to do? Are you going to call Chief Karlman?' Mac asked.

'Maybe when I figure out what it means – if I figure out what it means. I'm really not in the mood for Karlman's we'll-get-around-to-it attitude right now.' He noticed Mac was hefting the key up and down in her hand. 'What?' he said. 'What are you thinking? You look like you're thinking something.'

51

Mac hefted the key a few more times. 'Do Mother and Dad still have that safe deposit box over at Connecticut Federal?'

Chad shrugged his shoulders. 'I guess so. Why?'

'Have you ever gone with them when they went to the safe deposit?'

'No. Why?'

'I'm not sure, but I think it had a weird key like this.'

Chad pushed back his chair and stood up. 'It did? Well, let's go!'

'Easy, Chad. You finish your coffee and I'll go change into something more presentable for a bank visit.' She plopped the key back down in front of him, on top of the mail. 'Besides, Mr New Business Owner, it looks like you have some bills to open.'

One of the advantages of living in a small town – a very small town – was that everyone knew you. Mac had also realized, in her late teen years, that the very same thing was also one of the disadvantages of living in a small town. Today, however, they were enjoying one of the advantages.

Charles Corman, who handled the many Griffin accounts at Connecticut Federal, had been most helpful. No, the key wasn't to one of their safe deposit boxes. It was for one of the boxes at Registon Savings and Loan.

Jessie Jonathan was the bank officer on duty when they got to Registon Savings on the Boston Post Road. She was delighted to see them both. 'Mackenzie, how are you, dear?' Miss Jonathan said, extending both her hands and clasping both of Mac's. Miss Jonathan wore a sensible banker's suit, and a silvery scarf around her neck that complemented her silvery hair. Unfortunately, she wore a bit too much frosted eye shadow which gave her face a silvery look as well. 'We've been hearing about you, you know. Dribs and drabs only, but about you and that nice Rossellini fellow. I assume he's nice or you wouldn't be seen with him, right?'

She turned to Chad and took one of his hands. 'And Chadwick, we're so happy to hear that you're taking over River's End, and we trust you'll be keeping the accounts with us.' Having gotten her plug in, she suddenly remembered. 'But I just heard about Malcolm Howard this morning. Isn't this awful?'

'Awful, yes,' Chad and Mac concurred. Neither said anything more, not knowing just what it was Miss Jonathan had heard.

'Now, what can I do for you,' she asked as she led them to her desk and indicated the two guest chairs in front.

'I'm pretty sure I'm in the right place,' Chad said, pulling the key out from his jacket pocket. 'Can you tell me if I can get into this safe deposit box?'

Miss Jonathan looked at the key and took it from his hand. 'Let me check for you.' She went to the narrow file behind her and pulled out a drawer filled with individual trays of cards. 'A-34. Here it is.' She pulled out the bank card form, and folded around it was a standard sheet of paper. 'Oh, I see that Malcolm Howard was in and left authorization for you to be added to the signature card as an authorized user.' She took her seat and looked across the desk to Chad. 'I guess since you have the gallery now, that makes sense, since this was part of the gallery's accounts.' She looked down at the papers again. 'Strange, I don't remember Malcolm being in here last week. Oh!' she said, peering more closely at the sheet of paper, 'he was in here Saturday morning. That's why I didn't see him.'

Chad leaned over. 'He authorized the signature on Saturday?'

'Yes,' Miss Jonathan said. 'My, my. And to think he was dead by Sunday morning.' She stared at the paper for a few moments, then her voice resumed its usual perky business tone. 'Well, let's get you set up on the signature cards and then we'll get you into the box.'

Like most banks, Registon Savings had a small private room for box holders. Miss Jonathan left Mac and Chad there, once she'd placed the box on the table for them. It was a standard-sized box, the middle size of the three the bank offered. The tray of the box measured about nine inches across and perhaps fifteen inches deep.

Chad looked over the table at Mac. 'Ready?'

'Go for it,' she replied.

Chad opened the top of the tray, and started piling the items onto the table, identifying them as he did. 'Looks like the original of the deed to the gallery lot. Yep. I saw a copy at the closing. Next is the back-title search on the gallery building, going back to . . . 1803, I think Howard said. Here is a copy of the contract with Alan Gerber – he's that artist over in Albany I told you about.' He paused and looked up at Mac. 'Exciting so far, isn't it?'

Mac smiled at his impatience, a character trait of Chad's since childhood. 'Go on,' she said, 'there's more.'

'Here's Malcolm Howard's passport, which I'm sure he

forgot he put in here. Another contract, this time with an
artist out in Michigan that he told me about. And—' he
peered more closely at the remaining paper in the drawer,
apparently the last. It was a standard 8½ × 11 inch form, with
a blue logo design at the top, and had been filled in in
handwriting. Chad picked it up to inspect it more closely; as
he did so, they could both see it was the last item in the box.

'What's this? It's a contract for a storage unit in New
London. Unit 113 at Old Colony Storage. Signed almost
three years ago' – he flipped the pages up – 'and renewed
two years ago, last year, and in September.'

'Look on the back, Chad,' Mackenzie said.

He flipped the pages over. There was a key taped to the
bottom page, the most recent contract form. 'Another key?!
Damn! This is turning into a treasure hunt!' He sat back with
a sigh, and started putting the other items into the safe
deposit, piling them in the same order they'd been in before.

'So how about I buy you lunch in New London?' he said
to Mac as he got up from the table, holding the drawer under
his arm.

'Sounds good to me.' She followed him out the door.

Before they got back to Miss Jonathan, Chad turned to
Mac. 'If we get to this storage place, and there's another box
locked up there with another key in it, I just want you to
know that I'm not responsible for what I might say – or do.'

'Gotcha,' Mac replied with a smile.

They decided they'd go to the storage building first, and have
lunch later. Which turned out not to be a great decision,
food-wise. But that wouldn't be evident for hours.

They took the interstate to New London, getting off at the exit nearest the railroad station, since the address of the storage facility seemed to place it in that section of town. Coming off the highway the exit curved up a hill and afforded a view of New London and its harbor that Mac had always loved. For a few seconds, if you blocked out the automobiles, and the power lines, and telephone poles, and concentrated on the buildings and on the river that fed into the Sound, you could transport yourself back to when New London was booming – around 1820 or so. It had been known as the Whaling City, and its port on the river Thames (pronounced *Th-ames* here, not *Temz*) was one of the busiest in the early days of the republic.

They passed the renovated train station, and after a few turns found themselves on Washington Street. Ahead on the left was a large building, painted in a now-peeling white; freshly painted over the white were large green letters identifying it as Old Colony Moving And Storage. Underneath the name it said 'Weekly – Monthly – Yearly Storage Available'. A third line, in smaller letters, said 'Ask About Our Temperature Controlled Units'. A fourth line, in a size almost as large as the name, gave the phone number.

They parked alongside the building. As Chad and Mac walked to the front door, he seemed to be sizing up the neighborhood. 'Not bad,' he said, 'not great either, but not bad.' Mac looked to see what prompted his comment, but she couldn't tell. As far as she could see, it was your standard industrial area.

The lobby area was dim, since it was painted in a dark gray and lit by a single bulb in a central ceiling fixture. There

56

was a windowed office to the left, and a security glass that slid back. The glass slid back now, and a man in his mid-thirties popped his head up. 'Hi, folks, what can I do for you?'

Chad stepped up to the window. 'I'm here to see . . .' No, that wasn't right. 'I'm here for . . .' That wasn't it, either. He pulled the key out of his pocket. 'Unit one-thirteen,' he finally said.

The guy eyed him suspiciously. 'Fine, we'll just get you signed in here.' He spun around the clipboard with the sign-in sheet, and flipped over the ballpoint pen that was attached to the top of the clipboard with a cord. 'One-one-three, you said?'

'That's right,' Chad replied. He glanced back at Mac with a raise of his eyebrows. Maybe it was going to be easy to get in.

'I'll have to see some i.d.,' the fellow said through the window.

Chad pulled out his wallet. 'It's a DC driver's license. I just moved back last week.'

'That's good. Just so long as I see your picture and signature.' The guy leaned back and picked up a piece of paper on the far side of his desk. 'Mr Griffin, it is, right? Oh yeah, Mr Howard left a note Saturday to add you to the signature card.'

'Saturday? Mr Howard was in here Saturday?' Chad asked. Mackenzie had stepped to his side, and he looked down to make sure she was listening to this as well. 'Can I see that?'

'Sure,' the guy said, and handed the paper to Chad. This

one had been typed out, and it was dated Friday the first. It gave the details of adding Chadwick Griffin's name to the rental agreement, and Howard's signature was on a line on the lower right.

'Yeah, he was in here late Saturday morning,' the man continued. He picked up the clipboard and flipped back two pages. 'Signed in at 11:45, out at 12:05.' He put the clipboard down again, and turned it toward Chad. 'If you'll just sign on the next line, I'll get the card for this unit and you can sign it.'

Chad did as the man requested, and flipped back to look at the Saturday page himself. There was Malcolm Howard's signature, looking a little rushed, but definitely Howard's.

The card that the man presented to Chad for signature stated the current term of the lease – through next September 20 – and the monthly rent, which seemed a bit steep to Chad. Almost $200 a month. 'What's the size on this unit?' Chad asked.

'One-one-three's one of our biggest – ten by fifteen. Only three in the building. And it's on the side that's powered, so it's got the temperature control, too. 'Course the power is metered separately, and that's on a different bill.'

'Great,' Chad muttered under his breath. 'This is costing almost as much as my first apartment that year I went to summer school.' He signed the card and pushed it back to the other side of the windowed ledge. 'Now, how do we get there?'

'Take the elevator up one floor. Turn right, all the way to the end of the aisle. One-one-three is a corner unit – you can't miss it.'

Chad turned to his sister and they walked to the elevator together. 'I'm always suspicious of directions that end with the phrase "you can't miss it",' Mac said quietly.

'We'll pace the whole floor if we have to, but I'm not coming back down to ask directions from him again.' The elevator opened with a clang.

The elevator opened on the second floor with less noise, and they stepped into a corridor that was adequately lit. Chad turned to the right and took the lead. After a few steps, he slowed his pace, and Mackenzie caught up with him. The hallway was wide enough that they were able to walk side by side.

Suddenly Chad's gait slowed noticeably. Mackenzie looked at him and saw an odd expression. 'What's the matter?'

Chad came to a complete stop. 'I don't know. It all sort of caught up to me – everything that's happened in the last, oh, thirty hours or so. Howard dead, those guys beating the crap out of me' – he touched his cut eyebrow gingerly – 'getting a weird message in the mail, finding the key to this place. This is not the kind of life I normally live, Mackenzie.'

'I know that.'

'And a thought just occurred to me – do you think we're going to find something weird in here? 'Cause I tell you, I'm just about creeped out.'

Mac shrugged her shoulders. 'No way to tell until we open the door.' She looked up at him carefully. 'You want to take a break, go get something to eat first?'

'Nah,' Chad said. 'Might as well get it over with.' They continued down the hall to the end of the corridor.

Mackenzie counted off the last few doors. 'One seventeen.

One fifteen. Long space here – you can really tell it's one of the bigger units. And here we are. One thirteen.'

Chad fumbled with the industrial-strength padlock until he got the key going in the right direction, then beckoned Mackenzie out of the way while he swung open the wide door. Still standing in the corridor, he felt the interior wall on either side of the door until he found a light switch. He flipped it on and the darkened, closed room became brightly illuminated.

Chad still stood in the corridor, looking inside, and Mackenzie came up behind him and tried to peer over his shoulder. 'Any dead bodies or anything?'

'Mackenzie!' Some things never change between brothers and sisters.

'Well, let's go in then!'

They stepped inside. The door was placed in the center of the long wall, so the room was approximately ten feet deep ahead of them. At the far left end was a neat stack of wooden boxes in various sizes. Directly across from them was a larger stack of similar wooden boxes. At the wall on the right was a row of much larger wooden boxes, fewer in number, and quite shallow but substantial in height and width. Over in the farthest left corner sat a tank-like machine which had a small pilot light that glowed.

Mackenzie stepped toward the stack of boxes to the left. Keeping her hands in her storm-coat jacket, she nosed around, just taking in detail. She walked up to the machine first. 'Humidity control it says.' In New London, this near the water, that must mean a de-humidifier. She looked to the stack. 'These are all pretty rough boxes. Looks like rough pine –

that really cheap kind they sell at the lumber yard.' She looked back to Chad, who was still standing just inside the door. He nodded his agreement. 'And look at this, all these boxes have a green and a red mark on them.'

Chad stepped over to join her at that point, and inspected the marks she indicated. It did look like some substance – heavier than a marker, but not as heavy as paint – had been stroked on the top left of each box. By the time Chad got through looking, Mac was at the larger pile in the center of the room.

'These have just a green mark.'

'And do those things at the other end have just a red mark?' Chad asked.

Mackenzie stepped over to the rows of larger boxes. 'Nope. Black marks.'

'How the hell do you think we'll get these open?' Chad said, fingering the red-and-green marked boxes.

'We're probably going to need some tools or something,' Mac answered. As she did, she moved the front box with her index finger. It moved quite easily. As she bent down, she realized that it was so light because it was empty. 'Chad, look at this!'

Mackenzie pulled the box away from the others, and they saw that it was more a frame than a box. The four sides were solid pine, and the bottom, the part that had been facing them, was of even thinner material, closer to balsa wood. But the opposite side was just open. It had been propped against the next box, which was of similar construction. Only on this next one the open side of the box faced out, and they were looking at its contents.

A large rectangle, probably forty-eight inches wide by thirty-six inches high, was draped in a cream color waffle-weave cloth. Chad and Mackenzie exchanged quizzical looks, and, in an unspoken decision, Mackenzie moved the empty box out of the way while Chad pulled the cloth-draped object out.

Chad propped the bottom of the object on top of the other boxes and pulled the cloth off. 'Oh, my God,' he said.

'What? What is it,' Mackenzie said, turning back to him. She saw a beautifully framed painting – oil, she guessed, but she hadn't a clue about details like that – in what she would describe as a pastoral scene.

'I don't know if it is, but it sure looks like a Jasper Cropsey.' Chad didn't look at her when he spoke; his eyes raced back and forth over the painting.

'A Jasper Cropsey? Is that a real name?' Mac had lamented at various times her lack of education in the fine arts. Chad had often joked that it was a wonder anybody growing up in their house had developed any aesthetic sense whatsoever, since what passed for 'art' in their parents' home was any number of images – in drawings, prints, paintings, and wooden figures – of waterfowl, flying or paddling, living or dead. Though Mac hadn't followed in her parents' footsteps, her taste in art ran to twentieth-century poster art and photography, both of which were prominent in her apartment. And she had absolutely no idea who Jasper Cropsey was.

'Nineteenth-century American, one of the key figures in the Hudson River School.' He turned the painting so Mac could see it. It was beautiful, an explosion of fall colors, and

Mac could tell that the painting – a sunset scene of a hill that sloped down to a river, with palisades in the background – bore a relationship to the landscape of the Hudson River as she knew it. But the painting reminded her of depictions she'd seen of paradise, because the scene she was looking at was too idealized, too beautiful to be real.

'Cropsey was able to capture that quality of the Eastern sky,' said Chad, pointing to the painting for Mac's benefit. 'See the way the light is diffused, like it is when the sky is just a bit hazy from the humidity? But see how the trees and the river pick up the light, but not quite as brightly? That's Cropsey. And I think I have seen this, or its double, any number of times at the museum in Washington,' he finished.

'Really,' Mac said. 'So what do you think this is? A forgery? Or is it real?'

'Right now I can't tell.' He set the painting back into the box he'd pulled it from, and draped the cloth back over it. 'From looking at this, Malcolm left these things in pretty good shape; this is close to the kind of packing you do when transporting museum pieces. The waffle-weave cloth lets the items breath but keeps most of the dust off. That's being pretty careful with forgeries.'

'Why don't we open the others and see what else there is?' Mac said.

Chad carefully moved the box frame that contained the Cropsey, and propped it against the front wall of the room. In short order, he had removed the other five paintings from their boxes and propped them up on the stacks. It was mind-boggling.

Chad could feel his respiration increasing as he pulled the

paintings out, and when he saw them all together he couldn't help letting his mind run away for a moment. Was this going to be one of those great stories, like the person who'd bought a painting for the equivalent of a dollar at a flea market in the south of France and ended up with a Van Gogh? True, his purchase of Howard's gallery was a little more than a buck, but there was a possibility of treasure before his eyes.

'Chad, even I recognize two of these,' Mackenzie said. 'This,' she said, pointing to a seascape, 'is by that American impressionist guy . . .'

'Childe Hassam,' Chad filled in the name for her.

'Yes, that's the one. And this,' she said, pointing to the largest of the paintings, and the one he'd uncovered last, 'I mean, anybody who's bought a pretty calendar in the last ten years has seen this one. It's one of Monet's lily paintings.'

'No, it isn't,' Chad said firmly.

'It isn't?'

'That one I'm sure of. It's an out-and-out fake. But you can't even really call it that. It's a meaningless copy.'

'Why do you call it that?'

'There's no attempt to pass itself off as the original. The size is all wrong. The original painting is at least two and half, maybe three times the size of this. What this does is capture the image of Monet's painting, and it captures it pretty well, but I wouldn't call it a forgery.'

'What about the others?' Mac asked.

'I don't know,' Chad said with a shake of his head. 'I don't know.'

'Chad, did Malcolm Howard ever mention this storage space to you?'

'No, not a word.'

'Is there an inventory of any kind that was part of the sale?'

'Very minor. There are a couple of pieces locked in that safe that I showed you on Saturday. But the assets of the gallery were mainly the name, the location, and a few contracts.'

'Do you think maybe Malcolm was into some art thievery here?' Mac said gently.

'I don't know. To figure that out, we'd have to find out if any of these are real, and that's going to take some doing.'

Mackenzie looked toward the stacks of boxes. Most of those definitely had six sides to them. 'How about I go down and borrow some tools from the guy down at the desk while you wrap these back up? That way we can check what's in these boxes and then get some lunch. I'm getting hungry.'

The man in the lobby was able to find a hammer and screwdriver for Mac, and she was back in the storage room within minutes. When she returned, she found Chad had started on the next largest stack, the one that sat at the opposite end of the room. He'd pulled one of the flat boxes from the rear of the stack, and the painting he'd unwrapped was propped on top of the remaining crates. Chad squatted before it.

'I don't believe this,' he said to her as she came back into the room. Mackenzie stepped alongside him, then hunkered down so she was close to the same eye level. The painting was of a woman kneeling at a priedieu, her hands folded in a prayerful attitude. Behind her, through a large open window, was a garden in full bloom.

65

'Oh, it has that funny forced perspective. Early Renaissance, right?' Mac said, proud that she had recognized *something*. 'Paintings like this always looked to me like they were flat and full of depth at the same time. Like how flat her face and hands are, versus the depth in the garden. So what do you think this is? Do you recognize it?'

Chad kept studying the painting. 'I've never seen this canvas before, but I remember it from seeing slides. It's from Venice, late fifteenth century, maybe early sixteenth. I don't remember the artist's name.' He squinted and leaned closer to the lower right corner, where there was evidence of a signature. 'Can't make it out.'

'Can you tell if it's real?' Mac said in a whisper.

'Not for certain, but it sure looks real to me.' Moving his finger just over the surface of the painting, he pointed out details to his sister. 'Look at those striations on her face. That's aging of the materials, and that would be hard to fake. And up in the corner, at the white trim of the ceiling. Way over at the edge, there's a streak where it's suddenly much darker. It looks like somebody cleaned the surface of this painting, and missed the last bit. Unlikely in a forgery, I would think.'

Chad stared at the painting for a few more moments, then set it aside. 'Let's see what else we've got here.' He pulled out the next box, and instead of a painting pulled out a beautifully framed map that was under glass. Real glass, too, from the weight of it.

'Chad, this is beautiful,' Mac said. 'Look at the coloring on this.'

The map was beautiful, Chad agreed. The border was

filled with detail, and colored exquisitely. The caption across the top of the map read 'Toto El Mundo' – the whole world. The European continent sat in the upper portion of the map, with the 'Mediterraneo' taking its proper place as the center of the earth and of the map. There was quite a bit of detail filled in on North Africa through to the Middle East. A greatly abbreviated 'Orient' completed the right side of the map. At the bottom of the North African section the detail gave way to open space, and the words 'Terra Incognito' ran across the continent. At the left of the map, the Atlantic Ocean, unnamed here, was filled with curvy lines, which seemed to indicate it was unknown territory as well. Over at the far left, a small land mass was depicted, and across the land mass was the word 'Orient' again.

'Chad, am I seeing this right? This is a map of the world without North and South America?'

'That's right. But look at the date. 1473. They didn't know yet.'

'This stuff is amazing. I can't wait to open the rest of these things,' Mac said, turning to pick up the screwdriver and to grab a box for herself. Chad reluctantly set the map aside and joined her.

Mac had chosen the smallest box first. 'You said both of those items were fifteenth century, right, Chad?' she asked as she examined a small object in her hand.

'Right.'

'Well, I have something that's a fifteen too, but I can't tell what it is.'

Chad leaned over from where he was now sitting on the floor and took the item from her palm. It was made of metal,

67

silver probably, and heavy for its size, which was approximately four inches wide, two inches tall, and not quite an inch deep. It had a smooth flat bottom, but the top surface bore an ornate inscription. 'See there, where it says XV – it's the fifteenth of something,' Mac said.

Many of the letters were hard to make out, and they ran together so it was difficult to determine where, or if, words began and ended. But Chad spotted one detail. 'I don't know what it is either, but look at this. A-V-G-V-S-T-V-S. Augustus.'

'You mean Augustus like the emperors?' Mac said wide-eyed. 'Mother should really be here.'

'Maybe like the emperors, I don't know. Augustus was around the time of Christ, and this style of lettering is later, at least second century, maybe third.' He hefted the piece in his hand, and turned it to look at it from different angles. 'But *augustus* also means esteemed, or something like that. Maybe this XV is a date, and all of this text gives it a more specific date about some esteemed person. We'll have to find out.'

'You're going to have your work cut out for you, aren't you?'

'If I pull in all the experts I'm going to need to pull in, I'll be owing favors until the turn of this century, believe me.' Chad dropped the metal piece back into Mackenzie's hand, for re-wrapping. 'Only a few more boxes. Let's go.'

Mackenzie next unpacked what appeared to be a small hand loom, age indeterminable. She was just starting on what it seemed would be her last box when she heard Chad gasp. She scooted toward him once again.

He was holding a book. A very old book. The cover

looked to be of ancient leather in an earthy reddish brown. 'What is it?' Mac asked.

'It's an illuminated manuscript,' Chad replied. 'An honest-to-God illuminated manuscript.' Chad fingered the cover carefully, and his index finger traced the gold cross that decorated the front cover. 'Look at the gold leaf inside this cross. It's in amazingly good shape – there's hardly any flaking to it.' He opened the book carefully and turned the first few pages.

'Look at the color!' Mac exclaimed, as he turned to a page that seemed to be filled with a brilliant blue.

'They used to grind lapis lazuli to get that color,' Chad said as he turned the page reverently, taking in as much as he could of the rich black brush strokes that made every letter a thing of beauty. 'And if a manuscript is intact, the color is preserved because when the book is closed the pages aren't exposed to light and air.' He continued turning the pages, lost in studying what he held in his hand. 'Amazing,' he whispered.

'Can you tell what it is?'

He turned back to the first pages. 'It's either the Old or New Testament or both, because that's all they did.' He looked at the first page and studied the letters closely. 'If my memory serves, this would have been the dedication – to the abbott, or whoever, and the names of the monks who worked on it and – here,' he said louder, 'see this – *anno domini* – the year of our Lord, M-C-D-I-I. 1402, right?'

Mac nodded her head in agreement. 'So this is fifteenth century, too.'

'Un-hunh,' Chad said, while fingering the leather binding

of the book appreciatively. 'And just about fifty years before the printing press.' He opened the book again and carefully turned a few of the pages toward the end of the manuscript. 'It is the New Testament anyway. Look at this. *Evangelii Sanctii Secundum Joannis*. The Holy Gospel According to John.' He set the book back into its box with care. There was more to discover here.

'I'm impressed with your Latin,' Mac said, still looking at him. Then she returned to the box she was opening, the last in this pile. Another heavy one. And either she was getting tired, or her imagination was starting to run away with her, because she gave a little yell when she uncovered the head.

'What is it?' Chad said with a start, and came to her side immediately.

Mac handed him the whole box. He set it down atop some of the others and pulled out the weathered stone head, a half-human, half-animal face bearing an expression of excruciating pain. Streaks of black and collections of white spots appeared across the face and on the features. It gave Mac the creeps. 'What do you think it is?' she finally said to Chad.

He shook his head. 'It's a gargoyle of some kind. From the way it's broken at the back of the neck, it's part of a larger piece, but hard to tell what that was. Could have been on a monument, or a fountain of some kind, or even a church. Whatever it was, it was outside for a long time.'

'Maybe it was somebody's fifteenth-century garden scarecrow,' Mac said, shaking her shoulders to ward off the spirits. 'It sure would keep me away.'

It was well past lunchtime when they finished with the

second stack of boxes. Chad eyed the last pile and then looked at his watch. 'It's ten to two. You want to head out for some lunch and then come back and tackle this?'

Mackenzie shook her head. 'No, my hunger peaked about an hour ago. I'm beyond food. Why don't we just take a look and then head home?'

Chad finished re-stacking the boxes they'd just done and started on one side of the largest pile. Mac took the other side. Chad got his box open first.

'Well, we leaped back a few more centuries,' he said to Mackenzie. She was still struggling with the top on the small crate she'd picked. It seemed to be more securely attached than the others. Finally she gave up and looked over at Chad.

He was holding a black- and terracotta-colored vessel, over twelve inches tall and about that size around, which looked like a large vase with a handle on one side. 'What is it?' Mackenzie asked. 'And how did you get it open so fast?'

'Just pried the top up with my key. And it's called an oenochoe – a wine jug. Look at these figures around the center here,' he turned the piece carefully so that Mackenzie could see the many figures depicted in the scene. 'It looks like it's a wedding party or a family scene of some kind.'

'Chad, do you think this is real?'

'It looks pretty real to me, but I'm not exactly a Greek expert.' He gingerly replaced the piece in the box, replacing the hay-like stuffing that had surrounded it. 'Now I really want to see what's in these boxes. This is fascinating.'

The two of them sat on the floor side by side, pulling boxes down one by one and prying them open, looking and sounding like children on Christmas morning. The next few

71

boxes that Mackenzie opened were metal pieces – bronze, Chad said. One was a tall thin pitcher with a handle on it which, he informed her, was a lekythos, an oil vessel; the other a silver bowl, about nine inches in diameter, with an ornate gold-colored interior.

Chad, meanwhile, had unwrapped several small sculptures that he identified as statues of the god Apollo. 'Quite anatomically correct for a god, don't you think?' Mac asked with a goofy leer.

As Mac was busy with her next box, the largest she'd opened, she heard Chad give a long, low whistle over his latest finding. She scooted over nearer him, and saw that he was holding an almost life-size head of a man. A very beautiful man. Even to Mac's untutored eye, she could tell the piece had the remarkable, classic proportions that characterized much of ancient Greek sculpture. But while many of the pieces ended up seeming cold or lifeless, this one had a warmth to it, a human quality that was immediately affecting. The curls in the hair tumbled as though blown by a recent wind, and the relaxed expression on the face looked like the young man had been interrupted mid-story.

'What do you think?' she asked Chad.

He didn't answer for a moment. He was too busy taking in the detail, slowly turning the piece in his hand, trying to observe it from every possible angle. It was of marble, and there was damage – a small piece out of the nose on the left nostril, a hunk missing from the ear on the other side. And from the once-jagged edges on the neck, the head had evidently sat atop a whole body at one point. The passage of

72

time had left many surface blemishes on the marble, but they managed to enhance the beauty of the piece. 'I think this is one amazing piece.'

'Anybody we know?' teased Mac.

Chad answered her seriously. 'See the wreath that you can spot under the hair? If it's only leaves, it's hard to tell, but' – he turned the piece one way and then the other – 'with those clusters of grapes, it means it's a head of Dionysus.'

'Grapes? So he'd be the god of wine?' Mac asked, looking at the statue more closely.

'Yup,' Chad replied. 'As in Dionysian revels.'

'But I thought Bacchus was the god of wine – as in Bacchanalian revels.'

'That's what the Romans called him. This is Greek.'

'I've always got those mixed up. Ares, Mars, Neptune, Poseidon – I can never keep them straight.' Mac shifted back toward her pile of boxes. 'Mother would be most distressed to hear this conversation.' Growing up with a mother who was a professor of classics should have cemented a little more of this into her brain.

'I won't tell if you won't,' Chad promised.

'Deal,' Mac replied.

In the end they had unpacked twenty-nine of what appeared to be ancient Greek and Roman artifacts. As Mackenzie put her last re-packed box atop the others, she turned to Chad. 'I have a real basic question. Did Malcolm Howard or the River's End Gallery deal in antiquities?'

'Not to my knowledge,' Chad replied with a rueful smile. 'Of course, what do I know? I only bought the business from the man five days ago.'

'Another basic question. Do you think Malcolm Howard was on the up and up?'

Chad heaved a sigh. 'Until five days ago, I would have said unquestionably. But since then, Howard's body showed up on the beach with a bullet in his head, and two gonzos tried to rough me up. Let's say I'm beginning to have my suspicions.'

'Speaking of your gonzos. Do you think one of these things is the *it* they were asking about?'

'Probably. But the jackpot question is, which one?'

'So what do you do with all this stuff?' Mac asked.

Chad re-arranged some of the boxes in the first group of paintings they'd looked at. 'I think I'm going to have to pull some strings and get somebody who knows something about Greek and Roman, somebody who's a fifteenth-century expert, and somebody who knows late-nineteenth and early-twentieth-century art cold to tell me what's real and what isn't. I have a strong hunch about the head of Dionysus. That feels real to me. And that fifteenth-century Venetian painting. That gets my vote right now as well.'

'And what do you do if this stuff is real?'

'One step at a time, Mackenzie. One step at a time.'

Mac looked at her watch. 'Yikes. It's after three. Let's get out of here. And if there's a hot-dog stand on the streets of New London, you're buying.'

FOUR

Tuesday was election day. It was an off-year election, or off-off-year as Mac called it, since it was only town and county matters on the ballot. She drove her parents to the voting place at the firehouse before breakfast, and returned to pick them up after she had picked up the *New York Times* at the drugstore.

When they returned home, Chad was already on the phone with Chief Karlman. From the expression on his face, the conversation wasn't going well. He replaced the receiver with a clang a few moments later.

'So what was his reaction?' Mac asked, handing him his coffee cup.

'He's not *convinced* that all that stuff we found in New London is related to Howard's death. Hell, I'm not *convinced* either, but let's check it out!' He took a mouthful of coffee, then set his mug on the counter and began pacing. 'But he did give me the name of one guy with the state police who works any art thefts that come up. I'm supposed to check in with this guy, then he and Karlman will confer, and *then* they'll decide if there's a connection.'

75

'But *you're* the one who has to call him?' This only confirmed Mac's opinion of Karlman's laziness.

'Yeah, but I'm going to go shower first,' he said, starting for the back stairs. He turned back, picked up his coffee mug again, and said to Mac, 'And remember, if you take the last cup of coffee, you make the next pot. You make sure she does, Stella.'

The housekeeper turned to him, her hand moving as though she were whisking him away. 'You best hurry with your shower, lad, if you're wanting your pancakes hot.'

Mackenzie had finished off her plate of pancakes and the first pot of coffee by the time Chad returned to the kitchen. 'So, Mac, can you head back to New London with me?'

'What for?'

'I just talked to the other guy with the state police. Sounds like a reasonable man. Says he really can't help me much unless we have some kind of detailed inventory of all those pieces, and the easiest way to do that is to take pictures. So I have to head back to the storage place, unpack everything again, take its picture and pack it back up. So are you game?'

'I can help you for a couple of hours, but I have to get a train back to the city this afternoon. I have seminars tomorrow and I'm having dinner with Sylvie tonight.'

'Sylvie the crazy actress? How is she?' Chad asked. 'I haven't seen her in ages.'

'She's still crazy. Working a little more, which is good.'

Their parents walked into the kitchen, obviously ready to head to the university. 'I just talked to Reverend Whitcomb,' Walker Griffin said. 'Malcolm Howard's funeral is scheduled for tomorrow. I told the reverend that you and I would serve as pallbearers, Chad.'

'Of course.'

'I know you have to get back into New York, Mackenzie, but the rest of us will be there,' their father finished. He stepped over to his daughter and kissed her atop the head. 'Safe travels.'

Her mother came around to Mac's side of the table as well and kissed her on the cheek, then wiped off the color her lipstick had left. 'It was wonderful to have you here for four whole days, dear, even if it did turn into a ghastly weekend.'

Mac got up to walk her parents to the door. 'I'll talk to you later in the week,' she said, waving as they started down the driveway.

When she turned back to the kitchen, she saw Stella placing a full plate of pancakes in front of Chad.

No, it was too disgusting to think of. She'd just had a full plate. But Stella's blueberry pancakes were so good. Well, maybe just this once . . .

'Hey, Stella, is there any batter left for seconds?'

Mac got back to her apartment after five that afternoon, barely an hour to spare before she had to meet Sylvie at their favorite restaurant.

There was a message from Peter on the answering machine. 'Mac? Are you there?' his voice echoed in the room. 'Mackenzie? It's Monday morning about seven o'clock in Nagano, and they keep telling me there's fourteen hours difference between here and New York, but I haven't been able to figure out if that means it's late Sunday afternoon or Monday night in New York. My head got totally messed up when we passed the international date line. Anyway, I just wanted to say hi. The tour's going well so far. And I miss you.' There was a noise in the background, like someone interrupted him. 'Gotta go, Mac. I'll try you later in the week. Take care.' It sounded like he planned to end the one-sided conversation there, then changed his mind. 'I really miss you,' he added.

That left a smile on Mac's face that lasted through the evening.

Before her first class on Wednesday, Mac managed to call Lieutenant Mario Buratti. He'd been her most frequent contact at the NYPD over the last few years, but their relationship actually went back to Mac's very first seminar for police professionals which she'd conducted as a green twenty-five-year-old newly graduated doctor of psychology. Buratti, who looked like a grizzled police veteran even at that point, had been thoroughly professional and even supportive of her through that experience. In turn, he'd won her loyalty. In the years that they'd worked together, Mario Buratti's was one of the professional friendships that Mac had come to prize.

The lieutenant picked up the phone on the first ring and barked 'Buratti!' into the line.

'Mackenzie Griffin here, Mario. You sound like you're either underworked or overworked. Which is it?'

'Depends why you're askin', Doc. So how are you? Haven't talked to you in a while. But I hear you're still seeing my *paisan*, eh?' Buratti took great delight in the fact that he was the one who'd brought Mackenzie and Peter Rossellini together, even if it was in the context of a case.

'Nothing gets by you, Lieutenant. That's why they pay you the big bucks.'

'So to what do I owe the honor of this call?'

'I think when we last consulted the favor bank, I was up about twelve. It's time to cash in a few.'

'Oh-oh, this sounds serious.' Buratti's cop voice was taking over. 'What's up?'

Mac did a brief recap for him of Howard's death, the assault on her brother, and their discoveries in New London. 'So what can I do for you, Mac?'

'Chad should be in the city by tomorrow. I thought maybe you could point us in the right direction toward a few people. I know the NYPD had a special art unit, maybe they still do.' One could never be sure in these days of city-wide belt-tightening. 'And maybe just listen to what Chad finds out up in Connecticut and tell us where the holes are.'

'You got it. I'll make a few calls this morning, talk to you this afternoon. I only worked with Norm Jarvi once and that's goin' back a few years, but I got on real well with him. I'll give him a call. Where can I reach you at, say, three o'clock this afternoon?'

It was Wednesday. This was easy to figure out. 'I'll be in my office.'

Dr Mackenzie Griffin's first class on Wednesdays ran from ten to eleven-thirty; then she had a half-hour break, during which she usually gulped down a fruit yogurt, and then her seminar with a dozen active-duty police officers which ran from noon to two. She normally held her office hours on Wednesday as well, making herself available to students until four o'clock, which was why she'd been able to tell Buratti so easily where she'd be.

Today had a slight departure from the usual schedule, however. Right after today's seminar, she was determined to get to the administration office and have it out with whoever had come up with this latest bit of bureaucracy she held in her hand. She had casually asked for an easel, a pad of 24 by 36 newsprint and colored markers, typical supplies for a discussion leader. Last week, just before she left for the weekend, she got three copies of the 'Request for Issuance of a Purchase Order' which she now held in her hand. Three forms for three items, rather common-place items at that, seemed a little excessive.

She waited for the elevator on the first floor, remembering the line that the elevators at John Jay's main building were as slow as they were big. And they were enormous elevators, with doors that opened in front and back. In her first year here, one of the instructors in forensics had joked in a crowded elevator, which a few people were attempting to make even more crowded, that, while the elevator was almost big enough for two caskets – and plenty roomy for one, not one more person could fit.

The door opened slowly and loudly, and Mac stepped aside while the passengers got off. She'd been waiting for the elevator by herself, and she walked to the opposite side of the car, where she'd be getting off on the fourth floor, and pressed her button. Just as the doors were closing, she heard somebody get on the elevator behind her, but they were apparently going to the second or third floor, because they stayed on that side of the car.

She started rehearsing her speech regarding the purchase orders in her mind, but as she did she noticed the aroma of men's cologne wafting her way. Heavily. This wasn't cologne somebody had splashed on; you'd have to bathe in it to get this concentration. Her eyes were almost stinging. Thank God this wasn't a subway car.

Suddenly she heard a click, and the elevator jolted to a stop. Simultaneously the lights went out, and Mac remembered hearing survivors of New York's blackouts saying there was nothing darker than the inside of a powerless elevator car. At this moment, she tended to agree with them. She reached her hand toward the button panel, hoping to find the emergency phone. In the dark, someone grabbed her hand. She screamed.

'*What?!* Oh, my God, you startled me,' she said, trying to pull her hand away from the hands that held it. They didn't let go. 'What are you doing? I was just trying to call the guard downstairs.'

Suddenly, there was a person behind her as well. The one in front still held her hand, but he was stepping to her right side now, and moving her arm around to her back. The person behind her stepped to her left side, and she had no doubt that he was the source of the cologne she'd smelled only moments ago.

'Nothing wrong with the elevator, lady. We just wanted a chance to talk with you, private-like.' This was the one on the right talking to her.

'What do you want?' she asked, hoping they wouldn't

hear the noise her pounding heart was making in her ears.

'We want you should tell your brother that his lordship wants what's his, and he's gonna get it.' This came from the one on the left, the one who went through gallons of cologne a month.

'But—' she started, hoping to explain that her brother didn't know what they were asking for. The man holding her arm cranked it toward her back more, however, and the pain stopped her from talking.

The one on the right spoke again; he seemed to be in charge. 'Look, lady, he wants the belt and he wants it now.'

Belt? What in the world were they talking about?

'Now you be sure to tell him, just like we told you,' the one on the right finished up. She started to nod, then realized they couldn't see her any better than she could see them, so she said 'Yes, I w—'

That's when the pain exploded on the left side of her head, and everything went white.

Mac woke up only a few minutes later, when the chief maintenance engineer checked on why the elevator had gone to the basement. The basement wasn't a public floor, and the elevator almost never came down here during the day. When he keyed the door open and saw Dr Griffin crumpled on the floor, he shouted for assistance.

Mac had started coming to, but when she touched her head, the chief was insistent she should not move until they got a stretcher down from the infirmary. Mac started to say that wasn't necessary, but when she tried to sit up she suddenly became more cooperative.

Twenty minutes later, when the infirmary nurse inspected her head, and announced she was going to Roosevelt hospital emergency for X-rays, Mac started to protest again. 'Do what she says, Mac,' a friendly voice said. 'In fact, I'll walk you over there myself.'

'How did you get here, Mario?' Mac said. 'Or is it such a slow day they're sending out lieutenants when a couple of guys conk somebody on the head?'

'These couple of guys happen to be the same ones who got your brother?'

'Yeah,' she said, squinting toward him. 'And let me tell you, they're beginning to piss me off.'

He had to bite back a smile. Lt Mario Buratti had known Mackenzie Griffin for almost seven years now, and, like anybody who spent any time with Dr Griffin, he knew that she considered profanity the sign of a weak vocabulary. These guys must *really* be pissing her off.

The impulse to smile died quickly, though. He didn't like what he saw when he looked at her. Blondes always looked pale to him; like his mother used to say, they looked like under-baked cookies. But she looked ghostly. And her eyes weren't as snappy as usual.

Mac looked at him, still squinting, and adjusted the ice bag on the back of her head. 'Mario, is this head trauma distorting my vision, or have you put on some weight?'

'Put on, and hope to God have started to take off. I quit smoking on Labor Day—'

'Congratulations,' interrupted Mac.

'No congrats necessary, believe me. It wasn't totally my idea. Gloria and the kids told me I'd have to start living on the screened-in porch if I kept on smoking. So stopping seemed the better of two alternatives.'

'So?' Mac coaxed, knowing there was more to the story.

'So I apparently set a new record by gaining twenty-two pounds by October fifteenth.'

'Your doctor must have been thrilled,' Mac said slyly.

'Hard to tell who was more thrilled – the doctor or Gloria. So anyway, as of Monday, October twenty-eighth, you're looking at a member of Weight Watchers.'

The idea of Mario Buratti at a Weight Watchers meeting made Mac want to burst out laughing, but she knew that would be interpreted badly. She managed to bite the inside of her lower lip, and put her head down, pretending to adjust the ice bag again. When she thought she could trust her voice, she asked, 'So how have you been doing?'

Buratti stared at her, knowing her well enough to know that she wanted to bust a gut, but he pretended they were having a normal conversation. 'Down five pounds in eight days on the Quick Start program. Only seventeen more to go.' And that was the end of that conversation as far as he was concerned. He turned to the infirmary nurse. 'So how is she?'

'Probable concussion, but I don't think it's severe. But it's a good idea to get her checked over at Roosevelt.'

'Okay if she walks over or do you want her in a wheelchair?' The hospital was directly across the avenue from the college, so walking was actually the quickest alternative.

Mac adjusted the ice bag again, trying to make sure it didn't get her hair sopping wet. 'No wheelchair necessary.

84

And *she* would appreciate it if you didn't talk about *her* in the third person.' She scooted to the edge of the examining table and hopped down. She winced as she hit the floor, and she saw that Buratti had caught it. 'So I'll walk over to the hospital, and then I'll take a taxi home.'

'Not necessary. Got a car downstairs.' He took her by the elbow and led her out the door.

It had been easier on the train. At least Buster had the smarts not to talk out loud when they were in public. But ever since they'd gotten back in the car, he'd been yappin' like a dog.

They'd left the car at the Yonkers train station and then rode the train into the city. Turns out it would have been faster to drive down the West Side Highway, but the old man was now very particular in his instructions about how they carried out this particular favor for him. And that meant following his orders to the letter, even when it woulda been faster to drive.

This part of Westchester always confused the hell out of Sonny, no matter how many times he drove around. Not that he was here all that often, but still, two or three times on a highway should make you pretty comfortable. But he always got confused about goin' from the Saw Mill River Parkway onto the Cross Westchester to 95 or was it the Cross County he should be looking for? That's the part that confused him. Cross Westchester and Cross County. It sounded like the same road to him.

Buster was as big a help as usual with his constant stream of chatter. This time it was about how maybe he'd move down to New York. About how he was ready for the big time, and the 'small fish' gettin' on his nerves. Yeah, sure, thought Sonny, you're about as ready for the big time as my Aunt Gracie.

Every once in a while Buster interrupted himself with a different version of the same joke he'd been telling ever since they pulled up to the corner across the street from that college. 'Maybe I should have a picture taken for my old man,' Buster had said when they were crossing the street. 'He said I'd never make it to college.'

His latest version was to turn to Sonny and say, 'Now we can tell people we went to college together.' He laughed just as hard at that one as he had the first twelve. 'Who'd a thunk that you and I would be in college together – especially a college for cops?'

Sonny grunted in response, since he'd learned that Buster would just keep repeating himself louder and louder until he got some kind of response. He hunched over the steering wheel to read the highway signs overhead. There! That's right, this is the one that would lead him to 95. He merged into the right lane and settled back behind the wheel. He hoped this afternoon's visit with the Griffin guy's sister would get them somewhere. The police still had a tight watch on the gallery and they couldn't get in there, and the old man was getting embarrassed that it was taking so long to do this 'simple favor'. He should only know.

For the second afternoon in a row, Mac returned to her apartment just after five. The emergency-room doctor at Roosevelt had taken X-rays, declared that she had a mild concussion, and warned her that she'd have a doozey of a headache for a couple of days, but that should be about the extent of it.

'Thank you Mario,' she said as they got in the front door. Buratti had not only eased her way through the emergency room, he'd entertained her with news of his children as they waited. Both boys were fine; Angela, however, was in the typical freshman-in-college phase of thinking her parents were uneducated morons who couldn't grasp the subtleties her freshman philosophy course required.

'It's like they should make it part of the school calendar, y'know, Mac?' Mario said to her as she sat, still holding the ice bag to her head. 'First there's orientation, then the first round of classes, then mid-terms, then it's your-parents-are-ignoramuses month. Or should I say ignoram-*i*?' Mac had to laugh at that, even though it made her head pound a little more.

After the doctor discharged her, Buratti had driven her home as well. It must have been a very slow day at the precinct.

'You gonna be okay? Anybody I should call?' he asked as he stepped into the living room, taking a quick glance around. He'd never had occasion to be in Mackenzie Griffin's home before. It suited her: fresh, nicely done, understated.

'No, I'll be fine. Do you need to call Gloria before you head out?' Mac liked Buratti's wife, and a healthier police marriage Mackenzie had never seen.

'Nah, I'm gonna head back to the station, turn in the car. I'll give her a ring from there.'

Almost on cue, the phone rang. It was her brother, frantic.

He'd called the school at three and the department secretary
had told him that Dr Griffin had been attacked in the elevator
and taken to the hospital.

Mac was able to calm him down, and determine that her
parents hadn't been alarmed. Then she told him about the
conversation with her attackers.

'Belt? What the hell are they talking about?' Chad said,
his voice still edgy.

'My reaction exactly.'

'And *his lordship*? Mackenzie, are you thinking what I'm
thinking?'

'There's only one lordship I know who's ever around
Registon,' Mac replied. 'Look, Chad, I've filled Lieutenant
Buratti in on the goings-on of the last few days, and he's
going to help us out to the extent that he can. Why don't I
put him on and you can tell him about your contact with the
Connecticut state police?' She handed Buratti the phone.

'Buratti here,' he said, all official. 'Yeah, nice to talk to
you, too. Yeah, so Mac tells me you were going to show
some pictures to the Connecticut state cops. Is that done
yet?' He paused for the answer. 'So you'll get them to their
expert tomorrow. Okay.' He reached to his inside jacket
pocket and pulled out his small notepad. 'And this Lord
Boleigh guy, anything you can tell me beyond what Mac's
filled me in on?'

He listened for a few moments, nodding as he did. He
tucked the phone in between his ear and shoulder so he could
jot notes. 'Okay. Listen, I've got some jurisdiction here
because of the attack on your sister. And I'm gonna milk that
for as much as I can. So I'll keep her posted. Right. Hey,

you're welcome.' Buratti thought that was the end of the conversation, but Chad obviously pulled him back in. 'Yeah, that's a good idea. She's in pretty good shape in this building, but I'll talk to the doorman on the way out.' He handed the phone back to Mackenzie. She tucked the mouthpiece into her shoulder and walked Buratti to the door.

'She's in pretty good shape meaning me?'

'Yeah. Your brother is worried about your security. He gets points for that, Mac. Anyway, I'll call you tomorrow and see how you're doing. And I'll arrange for you to talk to the art guy.' He turned when he got out into the hallway. 'Now you're going to do exactly what the doctor ordered, aren't you?'

'Absolutely, Lieutenant. Scout's honor.' She waited until he cleared the turn into the main lobby before she picked up the phone again. 'Chad? So how was the funeral?'

'Went off without a hitch. President Hutchinson did a nice job of pulling it off, I must admit. A few curiosity seekers outside the church, and the Hartford television stations sent crews down, if you can believe. Stephen Franklyn was in his glory.'

'Franklyn? He was there?'

'Pretending to be among the chief mourners. Talking about how he and Howard were colleagues, since after all they were both Riverside grads, Howard was in the art world, he was an art historian. He was talking to these TV crews like they were inseparable.'

'Refresh my memory, but isn't this the same guy who was sort of bad-mouthing Howard last Saturday night?'

'That's right. And I think you hit a hot button with your

tabloid comment. Stephen Franklyn-with-a-y seemed to know all these two-bit reporters by name, and he was dying to be interviewed by each and every one of them. I heard a British reporter down in Washington give his type a name. Media slut.'

Mac's head was pounding again, but there was one more thing she had to cover. 'So what is this that Buratti described as a good idea?'

'I'm going to put a security guard on the house here.'

'On Mother and Dad's house?'

'Yes,' Chad said, in a tone that let his sister know he would brook no argument. 'Look, Mackenzie, I've been attacked at the gallery, and you've been attacked at school, in another state for God's sake. We have no idea who these people are or what they're capable of.'

'Except we do know that at least one person is dead,' Mac added.

That almost took his breath away. Somehow Malcolm Howard's death had almost become disassociated from all the rest of this in his mind. There was the body on the beach, and then there was everything after. But it was one continuous line. 'Right. And if they know that I'm staying here, and they're still after me, and Mother and Dad and Stella are here . . .' his voice drifted off. He didn't want to finish the sentence.

'Chad, this whole thing is getting very scary,' Mackenzie said in a quiet voice.

Chad realized this was the first time in his life his big sister had ever admitted to him that she was scared.

FIVE

By ten Thursday morning, Mac knew she wasn't going to make her early afternoon meetings at school. The doctor had been absolutely right about the persistent and pounding headache, but the other symptoms he'd told her to watch for – blurred vision and nausea – had fortunately never shown up.

Chad arrived at Mackenzie's apartment late afternoon, as promised in yesterday's conversation. He was greatly reassured once he saw her, but started apologizing for bringing all this grief her way. Mackenzie tried to shush him.

'What really cracks me up,' said Chad, 'is the idea of all my friends congratulating me on getting out of scary ol' crime-ridden Washington DC and moving back to small-town America, where it'd be safe. Who can figure?'

Mac brought him a cup of tea from the pot she'd fixed for herself moments before he arrived, proof that she still wasn't feeling up to par. Mac was a coffee person, a full-fledged, grind-your-own beans coffee person. Tea was reserved for those occasions when she was in need of pampering.

'So what did you find out?' she asked as she sat on the

couch next to her brother, crossing her legs Indian-style. The meeting with the Connecticut state police art specialist had been this morning.

'We went over all the pictures.' He held up a couple of small bags full of Polaroids, showing her he still had the copies with him. 'But he's only going to do a comparison on the major pieces – mainly the paintings. What's been reported stolen, any similarities in terms of artists, that kind of thing. He knows the file well enough that he's sure none of the pieces we unwrapped are on their wanted list. And he says he doesn't have the resources to track down much with the Greek and Roman stuff, nor does he think it likely that he'd find much.'

'Well, it's a start,' Mac reassured him. She put her teacup down with a clank. 'Chad, I just remembered – what about the decorator and all the work you were supposed to get done before your opening?'

As tidy as the gallery was, Chad had decided to have the whole place repainted and some woodwork re-done before his grand opening, which had originally been scheduled for the weekend before Thanksgiving. 'I called her and re-scheduled for next week,' he told his sister. 'And I've put up a discreet little sign on the door that we'll be open that Saturday before Thanksgiving, but if we don't make it we don't make it. I can't very well have people working around there, or customers anywhere near the place, until we get this thing settled.'

Mac had to agree with him.

Mario Buratti showed up unexpectedly just a half-hour after

Chad arrived, and Mac was pleased to finally be able to introduce him to her brother. 'So, Doc, how you feelin'?' he asked.

'Are you checking up on me, Lieutenant?'

'You better believe it. Besides, I got a dinner down in the Village, thought I'd stop in on my way. So the head's better?'

'Yeah, getting better.' And it was. Mac had noticed an improvement even in the last few hours.

'Got a couple of other things for you. Got hold of Norm Jarvi at the art unit, and he's agreed to meet with us tomorrow morning at eleven. That okay with you?'

Mac and Chad looked at one another and nodded. 'With us?' she asked. 'You're coming with us?'

'Yeah. Can't say I'm in for the duration, but I'll be there to get you started, assuming the residents of the West Side don't start poppin' one another off, of course. And I found out a couple of other tidbits I thought you'd be interested in.'

Mac's face lit up. She'd been around Buratti's 'tidbits' before.

'I talked to your Chief Karlman today. What a meatball. Anyway, it seems in examining Malcolm Howard's financial records, they found monthly statements from Riverside Park, the rest home where his mother lived. You know the place?'

'I've seen it,' Mac said. 'It looks quite lovely. But I've never been inside.'

'Real top-of-the-line retirement home, apparently, from the almost five thousand dollars a month it was costing to keep her there. That was according to the statements they found. Strange thing was, they couldn't find any evidence of Howard paying it.'

'What?' Mac looked at Chad, then back at Buratti, as though she was missing something.

'The statements were there, in his name, and they showed receipt of this monthly charge, but there was no corresponding check or deduction from Howard's checking account.'

'Well it must have been from his mother's account, then.'

'They found those records, too, because Howard had power of attorney on that account. Not there either.'

Mac shrugged her shoulders, and looked at her brother. His face was as blank as she knew hers was. She turned back to Buratti. 'Wait. You said tidbits. What else have you got?'

'Well, among the canceled checks they did find, are monthly – sometimes more than that – checks in hefty amounts made out to one AC Brothers Three.'

'What the hell is that?' Chad asked.

'It happens to be one of the bigger, let us say, odds-making agencies in Atlantic City.'

'You mean bookies?' Chad said with a tone of disbelief. Buratti nodded yes. 'Bookies who take checks?'

'Technically, it's a legitimate business.'

'You mean there's a chance that Malcolm Howard gets in trouble with a bookie, gets killed and leaves *me* a note saying "He's got to be stopped"? Boy, was he barking up the wrong tree!' Chad sat back on the couch, eyes slightly glazed from the information he'd just taken in.

'I don't know that that's it, but I'll be able to check it out – tomorrow maybe, maybe later. I'll let you know what I find.' He patted his coat pockets as though looking for his cigarettes, then stopped himself. He looked at Chad with a lift of his chin, 'You had any more chance to think about this belt thing these guys were asking your sister about?'

'No, and I've been wracking my brain trying to figure out what kind of belt they could possibly be talking about,' Chad said. 'A man's regular leather belt? A money belt?'

'Like a money belt filled with money and maybe Malcolm Howard took it?' Mac asked.

Chad nodded yes.

'I don't think so,' she said as gently as possible. 'You knew him better than I did of course, but it doesn't strike me that Malcolm Howard was your out-and-out thief type, nor does it strike me that he was stupid. And anybody who would steal a money belt from these guys or anyone who had these guys working for him would be stupid.'

'So what other kind of belts are there?' Chad said, somewhat defensive. He thought the money belt had been a pretty good idea, actually.

'Well, you got your black belt,' Buratti said.

'And there's the Van Allen belt—' Mac started.

'What's that?' Buratti asked immediately.

'Radiation, I think. A band around the Earth. It has about as much to do with this as the asteroid belt. Or the Bible belt.' The three were silent as they tried to come up with something that made sense.

'Well,' Buratti finally offered, 'there's the belt of the heavyweight champion of the world, but somehow I don't think that would get big play in the art world.' He glanced at his watch. 'Listen,' he said, heading for the front hall, 'you guys keep at it. I gotta get going.'

'Where you heading for dinner?' Mac asked.

'It's a small retirement dinner, sort of the pre-official-dinner dinner, for one of the guys at Midtown South. We worked together up until maybe four years ago. He's one of the good guys. Besides, they're having dinner down at the Minetta Tavern – one of my favorite restaurants in the Village.'

'Is this on your Weight Watchers menu?' Mac said quietly as she walked him to the door.

'Nope,' Buratti said, almost gleefully. 'I'm looking forward to my first decent meal in almost two weeks, and I'm not thinking about calories, or fat grams, or nothing.' He paused once he stepped into the hallway. 'I'll see you tomorrow at eleven, right?'

Friday morning was gray and cold, and there was an occasional drizzle that hit the skin like pin-pricks, driven by a steady wind. Mac was glad they'd agreed to meet Buratti inside the main door of One Police Plaza, since it was not the weather to be hanging around on the street, as Chad's now inside-turned-out umbrella proved.

Buratti got them through the security check and led them back to the elevator bank, 'You'll like Jarvi,' he said as they waited for the elevator. 'Good guy. Knows what he's doing.'

'Have you worked with him?' Mac asked.

Buratti nodded. 'About eighteen months ago. What started out as an art-theft case turned into something a little more. It seems this artist came in and stole his own paintings back when he found out the gallery owner had been ripping him off. That wasn't enough for him, though, and he came back a few days later and killed the guy. Jarvi was on top of the case the whole time.'

Mac was glad Buratti was along to lead them through the circuitous corridors. After a couple of turns, he opened the door to a large office area, with a number of small, numbered offices off of it. Mackenzie assumed the whole area was the art-theft unit.

Buratti walked to an open door at the rear of the office area, the last door on the left. Mac followed, with Chad bringing up the rear; she had to stop quickly when she reached the door because there was virtually no space in the office. The room wasn't much wider than the desk it held; there was a standard filing cabinet in the right rear corner, and one guest chair, turned sideways, that sat in front of the desk. The top of the desk was almost covered with files and papers, as was the top of the filing cabinet. The piles appeared neat, and there wasn't an impression of messiness, just of too much stuff.

Detective Jarvi stood the moment Buratti walked into his office, and apologized after the introductions that there wasn't room for additional chairs. Mac insisted that Chad take the chair, since he had the 'show and tell' to do.

Chad, Mackenzie and Buratti filled Jarvi in on the details in a round-robin of storytelling, and he looked at a few of the Polaroids Chad passed to him. After they'd brought him up to date, he smoothed his jawline a few times, and sat back in his chair. 'I'll give you as much help as I can, but I don't know what that's going to be,' he said reluctantly. 'We're set up here for things getting stolen. This is the first time since I've been here that somebody's come in saying "look what I found".

'First, I got no registry of stolen objects,' he continued.

97

'We use the IFAR registry. I assume you've checked with them?' he said to Chad.

'Yes,' Chad said. 'A former colleague at the museum down in Washington gave me a name at IFAR, and I called yesterday or the day before. The only things I could identify with any precision were the paintings, and there was no record on any of them.' Jarvi nodded his understanding.

Buratti and Mac looked at one another. 'Okay, I'll bite,' Mario finally said. 'What's IFAR?'

'The International Foundation for Art Research,' Jarvi answered. 'Fifteen years ago, maybe more, they started keeping a registry of stolen art. A few thousand pieces a year are logged in with them, and there's probably more. It's a real help to legitimate dealers. If somebody comes in offering them a piece that's a little too rare, or at too good a price, they can call IFAR and check to see if it's hot. It's not a hundred percent, but it's a help. And when something's recovered, they log that in, too.'

'And how many times does that happen?' Mac asked.

'Recovery? Nationally and internationally, it varies. Ten to fifteen percent of the pieces stolen in a year will be recovered. Our record locally is a little better, actually a lot better percentage-wise, but it's like any crime. Your best shot is in the first twenty-four hours. After that, your chances start decreasing dramatically.'

'Norm, let me ask you this,' Buratti said, 'before we get started on all these other things. These guys who roughed up Doctor Griffin here, they were talking about some belt. Does that mean anything to you?'

Jarvi shook his head slowly. 'No. And it's an odd enough

term that I'd remember it if it came up on any of the stolen reports.' He looked off to the side, and then back to Buratti again. 'A belt? I wonder what the hell they're talking about.'

'How 'bout the name "His Lordship". That mean anything?'

Jarvi shrugged his shoulders. 'In terms of the legit customers in the galleries, I'm sure there are a few lordships sprinkled among them. If you're talking my side of the street, with the felons and all, no, doesn't ring a bell.'

Mackenzie edged a little closer to Jarvi's desk. 'This might seem a real basic question, detective, but I'll just go ahead and ask it. Why do people steal this stuff? Isn't it a little hard to turn this into cash?'

'On the major pieces, you're right, and that's what gets into the newspapers, so that's probably why you asked the question. But works valued at less than a hundred thousand or so, no. Many of those pieces aren't catalogued. Still, it's not the world for those interested in immediate liquid funds. You're not knocking off a convenience store here. That's assuming that financial gain is the motive, of course.'

'What are the other usual motives besides financial gain?' Mac asked eagerly. This was the part that was interesting to her.

'Lately, some of the major pieces that have been lifted in Europe seem to have a political motive behind them. Holding pieces for ransom, demanding the release of political prisoners, some terrorists, that kind of thing. One group even demanded that all the museums in England be closed down.'

Chad hadn't even heard of this one. 'What?' he asked. 'What's the purpose of that?'

Jarvi stretched back in his chair. 'Let me see if I can remember. They were insisting that museums were an imperialist exploitation of the poor nations of the world, and demanding that every object be returned to its country of origin. So I guess technically some of the museums in England could have stayed open if they only kept the English stuff.'

'A movement like that certainly would clear out the Metropolitan, wouldn't it?' Mac joked. 'We'd have a very large building on the edge of Central Park good for roller-skating.'

Jarvi nodded. 'But you have your other motives, too. One guy we finally picked up here a few years ago, he hit galleries mainly, not museums. He wasn't trying to sell the pieces he lifted, he just wanted to have them, be able to look at them. We found about eight hundred thousand dollars' worth of art in his apartment – a nice little one-bedroom out in Queens. And the only reason we caught onto him is one of the salespeople at the last gallery he hit saw him walking out with a sculpture under his arm. In broad daylight.' Jarvi shook his head at the wonder of it.

He continued. 'But money is your primary motive, that's for sure. And even with major pieces, you can score some pretty good money if you know what you're doing. A thief might only get about ten percent of the value, but if you've got a six-million-dollar painting, ten percent is a pretty good day's work.'

'Who buys something that hot?' Buratti asked. 'What cast of characters are we looking at here?'

'Some private collectors that let their acquisitiveness get

out of line. Interpol suspects that some of the big heists are commissioned. Instead of letting the local car thieves know you're in the market for a burgundy Mercedes, you put the word out that you want a painting by Van Gogh.'

'So Interpol's involved in this, too?' Mac said.

'Oh, yeah.' Jarvi reached to the left side of his desk, to one of the neat piles Mac had noticed before. 'These are the Interpol notices that have come in so far this month.' He turned and pointed to the larger pile that sat toward the front on top of the filing cabinet. 'That's last month's. Every once in a while you get real lucky. In the spring, a gallery owner up on Madison had both me and IFAR on a conference call, 'cause some guy had come in offering him the moon. It turned out the piece was on the Interpol notice that I received that morning. The gallery guy starts describing the piece to me, I start describing it right back, reading off the notice. The guy almost peed his pants.'

'Let me get back to the cast of characters,' Buratti said. 'I heard from one of the guys in narcotics that some of the real bad guys started dabbling in this.'

'True. Starting back in the mid-80s, I guess, when some of our South American friends really started bringing in the serious dollars, they were looking for a way to clean up some of their money. They're not necessarily on the theft side of things, though. It's just a good way for them to move money. If you've got ten million sitting in an account in Amsterdam, you cultivate a relationship with a gallery or auction house or whoever, you pick up a Brueghel for say seven point five million, you've got a legitimate bill of sale. And art passes through customs duty-free. So you've still got two and a half mil in the account, and you know you'll have even more next month, and you got a seven and half million dollar painting on your side of the border. And a Dutch masterpiece, to boot.'

'This is getting very depressing,' Mac said, shifting on her feet and finally leaning back against the wall.

'Hey, you're getting uncomfortable,' Jarvi said. It was easy to tell he was warming to his subject, and had absolutely no objections to continuing. 'Let me go see if we got one of the conference rooms available.'

When she saw the room they adjourned to, Mac wondered if conference room was now interchangeable with interrogation room in the new police vocabulary. It didn't look like there were any two-way mirrors, but at least there was a good-sized table with six chairs. They all sat down, Buratti and Jarvi on one side, Mac and Chad on the other.

'Let me tell you something about art crime,' Jarvi said as he got up to close the door. 'Art crime is the second biggest international crime – in terms of frequency of occurrence and the dollars involved – after drug trafficking. But it doesn't help that we don't get more attention. To deal with it, you got me, and one guy in LA. There was a guy in Chicago, part-time, but they cut back. And then you got the Feds. Now they recently increased their art-crimes staff by 400 percent, according to their press release, which means they got four agents working on it now instead of one. Three down in Washington and one here.'

'*You're* the art unit?' Mackenzie asked, very surprised. 'I thought you were in charge of the art unit.'

'Well, I guess I am in a way, 'cause I'm it,' Jarvi

responded with a bright smile. 'Part of the problem is, art theft is sort of refined, y'know?' He tilted his chair back, then slammed down the front legs. 'When I finally catch one of these guys and haul him into court, the judge is practically smiling that this jackass is in for lifting a Degas – instead of for shooting some eight-year old in a playground. It almost seems nice, y'know?'

Buratti nodded, like he knew exactly what Jarvi was talking about. 'Let me get back to the pool of likely suspects,' he said. 'Any chance of mob involvement?'

Jarvi shook his head no. 'Not here, not likely. There were hints the Mafia was involved in a couple of big heists in Italy, but that goes back a while.'

'How about Greek and Roman artifacts?' Chad asked. 'Much going on in that area?'

'Almost nothing at all, to be honest. Or nothing that I'm aware of. The vast majority of art theft in the States is in twentieth-century art. There are certain places where antiquities have been a problem – in the Middle East, down along the Mexican border with the pre-Columbian material, but so much of that is fake it's hard to tell the real impact. But with Greek and Roman, you're talking a real specific group of collectors. And the museums, of course.' He started looking at some of the pictures Chad had spread out before him, and he picked up one to look at it more closely. 'You said you might have an illuminated manuscript, too, right?'

Chad nodded.

'You know who you should see? The guy was an enormous help to me when I started in this six years ago. Knows more about more areas of art, and more of the nitty-gritty stuff, than anyone else I've ever come in contact with. He used to head up the sales over at Bartholomew's. Any serious collectors, legit or otherwise, whose interests cover all this material, he'll know about them.'

'Are you talking about Thomason Vandeveere?' Chad asked.

'He's the one,' Jarvi answered. 'You must know him then. Good.'

'I don't know him,' Chad answered. 'But I've heard of him. And my friend down in Washington suggested the exact same thing, that I talk to him, but I have no idea where he is.'

Jarvi smiled. 'He's in Santa Fe, and I'm sure you'll have to go there to talk to him. From what I've heard, you couldn't pry him out of Santa Fe with a can opener, especially not to get him to come back to New York.'

'So he's not with Bartholomew's any longer?' Chad asked.

'Technically, he's still on a leave of absence, and if Bartholomew's is smart, that's just the way they'll keep it. Either Sotheby's or Christie's would snap him up in a minute if Bartholomew's tried to strong-arm him. From my conversations with him right before he left, and from what I've heard since, it was just a bad case of burn-out. But I tell you this guy is amazing.'

Buratti cut in. 'You said the Feds have one guy working this here. Think we can count on him to help us with some information?'

Jarvi frowned. 'Hard to tell. You know that any contact has to be through local law enforcement, and it doesn't sound like your guy in Connecticut's going to help.'

Buratti slid his chair back. 'Maybe I'll go give him a call, say I'm working the case. And in a way, I am. There was that attack on Doctor Griffin here, y'know, after the alleged perpetrators had previously attacked her brother here in another state.' He headed for the door, then paused when he opened it. 'That ought to get him going. You know how it revs their jets when you talk about crossing state lines. I can use the phone in your office?'

Jarvi nodded with a smile as Buratti left. 'He's a good guy, y'know. Knows what he's doing.' He looked down at the photographs still arrayed before him. 'You know where the FBI could be of help to you, is heading you in the right direction to get these things tested.'

'I hope so,' Chad said.

'You mean you can get them authenticated?' Mac asked.

Chad looked at Jarvi. He shook his head no. 'It's just one of the quirks of logic that you can use testing to prove something is a fake, but it's almost impossible to prove that anything is genuine. That's been the point in developing the tests, to weed out forgeries. But the testing can help you rule out those things that are fake, and then you concentrate on the others, hoping you can come up with some kind of provenance for them before they came into Howard's possession.'

'Provenance?' Mac inquired, looking at the two men.

'Think of it like a title to a car or a house,' Chad said. 'A provenance is the history of ownership of a work of art, either from the time of its creation or, in the case of antiquities, from the time of their discovery. It lists the owners, where they lived, how long they had it.'

Buratti walked back into the room. 'The FBI will see us at two,' he announced to the room. 'Lemme ask you this, Norm,' he said as he resumed his seat. 'Daly just put it to me that it's unusual to have violent crimes – murder, aggravated assault like we got goin' here – associated with art theft. Is that true?'

Jarvi nodded his agreement. 'For the most part, yeah. You got your exceptions – like that case you and I worked on a couple of years ago. There's plenty of instances of museum guards or other security types getting roughed up a bit, or tied up. In fact there was a big robbery in Brussels last year, or maybe it was in The Hague, I'm not sure, where the museum's night watchman was shot and killed. But all those are in the context of the actual robbery. Things like you're describing – assaults, a murder away from the scene of the actual theft – it's very unusual. In fact I don't know as I've ever had a case like that.'

Buratti looked at Mackenzie with a raised eyebrow. 'I've got to hand it to you, Doctor Griffin. You come up with the quirky ones.' He put his hands on the table, palms down. 'Okay. Anybody interested in lunch in Chinatown?'

SIX

Jarvi ended up joining them for lunch, and Mac continued her questions about the world of art theft. She was fascinated that it occurred so frequently.

'Actually, it's under-reported, too,' Jarvi said over his helping of beef and broccoli.

'There's even more than you talked about?' Mac said. 'That's staggering. Why in the world wouldn't people report art theft?'

Buratti squinted across the table at Jarvi. 'Let me guess. Insurance rates.'

Jarvi gave him a thumbs up. 'That's part of it. Private collectors and even some museums can't keep up with the rate increases. Museums have the additional problem that they can't always keep track of where everything is, so they lose stuff.'

Mac look at Chad. 'Is that true? Museums lose stuff?'

'Sure,' Chad said, serving up more moo-shoo pork. 'Think of it. A small museum has objects that number in the tens of thousands. At a place like the Metropolitan, you're probably talking over a million. Between the exhibitions, what's on loan, what the lecture programs have out, not to mention the scholars' programs, there's no way to keep a really tight inventory control.'

'So why else is it under-reported?' Buratti asked Jarvi. He was trying to decide what he'd taste next – the lemon chicken or the sweet and sour.

'The Feds,' Jarvi replied. 'Not the ones you're going to see. The IRS branch. It seems some collectors don't want the IRS to know just how much discretionary income they had on hand when they purchased said missing art work.' He put his fingers around his teacup to see if it was cool enough to lift. 'Still, I can't tell if it makes my job easier. It's hard to imagine more thefts to deal with, but then again, maybe we'd start catching a few more of the pros in the field.'

Mac had a question she'd been wanting to ask. 'So, detective, if it's so much harder to sell – fence – these major art pieces for a good portion of their worth, why have we been reading about so many more thefts like that? We have, haven't we? I mean, it's not just my imagination?'

'I don't know that the ratio of major thefts has increased all that much, but ever since the mid-80s, when art prices started to hit the *Nightly News*, the goings-on in the art world have just received a lot more coverage. Anyway, if you're talking major pieces, you can still get a pretty high price, if you're willing to wait.'

'How so?' Mac asked, and Chad leaned over the table to listen.

'The Europeans started calling it "whitening". You put a stolen piece through four or five sales over the course of eighteen months, two years, bingo, you a have a new provenance. Usually, the ultimate owner is totally unaware that this piece developed magic legs eighteen months ago, so he sits looking at it in his den with a clear conscience. And some international law doesn't help either. In Japan, you can't recover a stolen piece if it's been more than two years since the theft. So if these guys bide their time, whiten a piece so that the new owner doesn't know it's hot, they're golden.'

Chad leaned on the table. 'How does one go about whitening?'

'What, Chad,' Buratti started razzing him, 'you lookin' to take notes in case you got to clean up some hot Greek vases?'

Jarvi picked up the ball nicely. 'I know more about how it's worked here, with lesser works, but I guess it's the same principle. First, you get a real bill of sale, maybe for a cheaper painting or a piece of sculpture that resembles the one you're covering up. From one of these estate sales or something like that. Plain receipt, no name on it. It just says bronze sculpture or painting of a woman and child. Now, say you're in New York City. You put the piece in an auction – maybe up in Albany, or Middlesex, or Chester, wherever you can find one of those small auction houses. You put it in the sale – under another name, of course – and then you buy it back again. This time in your own name. You get a detailed receipt, and bingo! You're legit.'

Chad sat back in his chair, nodding appreciatively at Jarvi's summation. 'Yeah, that could work,' he said.

Jarvi sipped his tea and turned his chair slightly so he could lift his ankle atop his knee. 'Actually I've given some thought to this. If I were going to be a thief, I'd be an art thief. It's fairly low risk – security is still shitty at most museums and galleries, not to mention the private collectors, and it's fairly high reward. Not a bad combination.'

Mac knew he was teasing. 'So how did you get the honor of being NYPD's entire art unit, detective?' she asked.

Jarvi warmed to the question immediately. 'You know, it's funny, when I was a kid – junior high, high school – I thought just about the coolest thing in the world would be to go to the Art Students' League on 57th Street. I always was interested in this stuff, but hey, life takes over.' He sipped his tea again. 'Anyway, right after I got my detective's shield, I was working drugs, drug trafficking. In fact the guy in this job before me, and the guy before him, all of us came out of drug trafficking. It helps 'cause sometimes you're running into some of the same people, like I said. This goes back about seven years now. One of the big cases I was working crossed over into some big-time art heist, and we did real well cracking that one. Anyway, I started working with the guy who was handling this desk then, and when he retired five years ago he recommended me and I got assigned.' He picked up his teacup again and winked at Mac. 'And at least now I get into the Art Students' League – for exhibits.'

'One last question, detective,' Mac said, glancing at her watch, 'and then it's break open the fortune cookies if we're going to be on time for the FBI. Earlier you said only ten to fifteen percent of stolen art was recovered internationally. What happens to the other ninety percent?'

'Occasionally we'll get lucky, and somebody will find some rolled up canvases in a dumpster someplace. But unfortunately most of it's apparently destroyed. If the thieves can't get rid of it, it's too hot to keep.'

They made it to the Federal Building with three minutes to spare before their appointment with FBI Special Agent William Daly. Mac had met a number of agents over the course of the last several years, and as they went through the usual introductions she was once again struck by how very similar they all were. Body language, speech patterns, inflection – all were eerily similar from agent to agent. She just had to get into the FBI training center as an observer at some point to find out what these people went through there.

Daly was in his mid-thirties and, looking at his still-crisp white shirt and still creased pants-legs, you would never know it was cold and humid and raining outside. He guided them to an interview room, and sat stiffly through Buratti and Chad's summary of the events that had transpired.

'And just what is it that you think the Bureau can do for you in this situation, Lieutenant, Mr Griffin?'

Buratti answered first. 'If you have any files on anybody who's been dealing in the type of thing we got here, we'd like to take a look. We need some help narrowing the investigation to people who are likely to traffic in these kinds of goods.'

'And?'

'When Doctor Griffin here was jumped in the elevator, these goons were saying how somebody they called His Lordship wanted his belt back. Do you know what they might have meant by a belt?'

'No,' Daly said.

This guy was getting on Buratti's nerves and the meeting wasn't a minute old. 'No idea. Okay. How about somebody called His Lordship? Does that mean anything to you?'

'No,' Daly said. Again, that was his entire answer. He looked at Chad. 'Is there anything else I can help you with, Mr Griffin?'

Like he's been a big help so far, thought Buratti. Fortunately he was able to keep the corresponding expression off his face. Or so he thought.

Chad ignored the expression of contempt on Buratti's face and answered Daly. 'I need your help determining what, if any, of the material I found in the storage locker in New London is authentic. If it's stolen, I want to return it to the rightful owners. If it's not, I'll take proper care until I determine what's going to be done with it.'

Daly drew cross-hatches on his legal pad while he spoke. 'I'm afraid the Bureau can't help you with the actual testing, Mr Griffin. We contract that out ourselves. I will be happy to discuss with you the tests I think would be most suitable for the materials, and for your goal of determining authenticity.'

'Fine,' Chad said, looking at Mac with a widening of his eyes that said 'can you believe this guy?'

'Let's address the paintings first,' Daly said. 'You said there were six?'

'Six in total,' said Chad. 'One I'm sure is a fake. But it's a bona-fide fake, if you know what I mean.'

'No, I don't,' Daly said flatly. A fake was a fake in his book.

'It's the wrong-size canvas, much smaller scale. It was an

attempt to get a pretty picture into a smaller space, that's all. I'm not worried about that one.'

'Very well. As to the others, a microscopic examination of the canvas would be first, especially around the signature area, which sometimes indicates a date as well. This detects micro-cracks in the paint, which are a natural result of aging. If there are no cracks, you have an incompetent forger, because some can be forced by heating. This area around the signature should be checked especially closely, because if there's a significant variation between the age of the painting and the signature, microscopic examination will detect it, This, like some of the other tests, is best done by a conservator or restorer, of course.' He finished with a practiced smile.

'Like solubility testing?' Chad asked. Daly nodded.

'What's that?' Buratti asked.

'You take a very small piece of paint and treat it with different test chemicals to make sure it behaves with the characteristics paints of that era are supposed to have,' Chad explained

'It's related to polarizing microscopy,' Daly said offhandedly.

'And what the hell is *that*?' Buratti said with a little more emphasis. This guy was *really* getting on his nerves.

'The expert examines a small paint sample under polarized light, which reveals pigment characteristics,' Daly said. 'A number of pigments weren't invented until the late nineteenth or twentieth centuries.' He looked to Chad as if to get confirmation of what he was saying, and he got it. 'Therefore if you've got a painting purporting to be from the sixteenth or eighteenth century, or even up through the nineteenth century, and it has one of those pigments included, you know it's a fraud.'

'Any other tests?' Mac asked, wondering if she really wanted an answer.

'Another that's available through expert analysis only. Infrared reflectometry.' Buratti's eyes rolled when he heard the term. 'An image of a painting exposed to infrared light is transmitted onto a video screen. The trained eye can detect inconsistencies in the paint, earlier restorations, perhaps earlier cleanings, sometimes even paintings that exist under the paintings.'

'*Pentimento*,' Mac said.

Daly and Buratti both turned to her. 'What?'

'That's the term they used for when a painter painted over a canvas,' Mac said, unaccustomed to being the one answering a question on art terms. 'I think it means "repentance" in Italian. I've always thought it was a wonderfully evocative word.'

Daly paused a moment to make sure she was through, then he turned to Chad. 'For the other items in your collection, Mr Griffin, I'll have to consult with my colleagues in Washington to see what tests we can recommend for you to establish their authenticity. I'm not as well versed in the other areas. And I'll put together a list for you of the laboratories that we deal with that do this kind of testing.' He moved his chair back to rise. 'One other thought. Given the wide range of style and media you're dealing with, I'd suggest you contact a gentleman who used to be, perhaps still is associated with, Bartholomew's. His name is—'

Chad interrupted him. 'Thomason Vandeveere.'

As they walked through the lobby of the Federal Building, Buratti could tell there was something on Mac's mind. They'd worked together enough that he could see it in her face. 'So what's on your mind, Doctor?'

Mackenzie slowed and finally stopped, stepping out of the way of the people heading for the elevators. 'All this talk about stealing. What if it isn't stealing, but more replacing?'

Buratti and Chad both said 'What?', looked at each other and then at her.

'No, think about it. What has to happen for a theft to occur?'

'Whaddya mean?' Buratti said. 'Somebody has to take something.'

'True, somebody has to take something, but it has to be reported. If nobody reported it, how would you know there's been a theft?'

'Doc, is this one of those tree-falling-in-the-woods kind of discussions?' Buratti said, squinting his eyes at her.

'Think of it. All this material that you've discovered, Chad. None of it apparently missing, at least from what the police and FBI and this IFAR registry can tell you. But what if nobody's reported it?'

'Why wouldn't it be reported?' Chad asked. He thought he knew where his sister was leading with this, but he wasn't sure. 'I don't think any of these pieces fall into the categories that Detective Jarvi was talking about.'

'I think there are a couple of possibilities. A, they're in on it which, given the number of items and the different places they must have come from, is unlikely. I don't think you get that many people to keep their mouths shut. I think B is more likely – they don't know.'

'They don't know?' The two men again echoed one another. 'Wait,' Buratti said. 'Who doesn't know?'

'The owners – the museums, the collectors – don't know these works are missing,' she repeated. 'Earlier, Chad, you were talking about how museums lose things just because they have so many of them. Think of how much easier it would be to lose something if there was no reason to suspect that it was missing.'

'Come again?' Buratti said.

'Am I right, Chad, that the only time a museum would inspect something for authenticity or research its provenance is when they acquire it?'

'Yeah, and on major pieces when they travel, but that's at the insurance companies' insistence, I'm sure.'

'So, major pieces aside, if you slipped an exact duplicate – a very good forgery – into a museum when you lifted the original out, what are the chances of it being found out?'

Chad pursed his lips and nodded slowly. 'Assuming you got away with the switch, almost none.'

Buratti whistled through his teeth. 'Very good, Doctor. I'm impressed.'

SEVEN

When Mac learned that Chad was taking the Metroliner down to Washington Friday night and wouldn't be returning until Sunday, she decided to do a one-day trip to Registon to see how her parents and Stella were holding up.

She was pleased when she checked on the security Chad had arranged. The men appeared quite professional, but were unobtrusive enough that her parents seemed unaware of their presence. Then again, her parents were frequently so wrapped up in their respective historical studies, they seemed unaware of the twentieth century.

The security people had not escaped Stella's attention, however. While she did concede the necessity of having them around, given what had transpired in the last week, she told Mackenzie that she didn't care to have these 'strrangerrs skulking about'.

Mac returned to the city on the late afternoon train, and got home just before seven, to find that she'd just missed yet another call from Peter. He was calling from Seoul this time, and made a couple of bad puns on the city's name. When the phone rang again at quarter to eight, she jumped to answer it.

'You don't have to sound so disappointed,' her brother said.

'Sorry, I thought you were going to be Peter.'

'Apology accepted, I think,' Chad replied. 'Listen, can you check your schedule and see what's up early Tuesday morning through Wednesday night?'

'Why?'

'Karen, my friend from the museum I told you about, she knows this Tom Vandeveere and got hold of him this afternoon. It's kind of bad news and good news.'

'How so?'

'The bad news is that he doesn't know anything about a belt either, but the good news is that he's agreed to meet with us on Wednesday in Santa Fe.'

'That will be a help,' Mac said and then paused as she mentally reviewed her calendar. 'Tuesday's okay, but Wednesday means shuffling a couple of classes around.'

'Can you do it, Mac? It would really help to have you there.' Then the tone of his voice changed and Mac could tell she was in for some brotherly cajoling. 'I can handle the art side of the discussion, but when it comes to the devious stuff you're so much better at that.'

'I think that was a "gotcha",' Mac replied. 'Okay, I'll make some calls on Monday.'

'Great,' said Chad. 'Karen and I are going to head out to dinner, and then I'm on the train first thing in the morning. I'll call from home with information on the flights, but I think we leave at the crack of dawn on Tuesday.'

Mac was able to move her seminar from Wednesday to

Friday, and she got someone else to cover her morning classes. She remembered to call and leave Sylvie a message on her answering machine, postponing the tentative plan they'd made to go to a new exhibition at the Museum of Folk Art. She even placed a call to Rachel Bennet, Peter's manager, to explain the circumstances, and asked her to let Peter know the next time she talked to him.

She made it home by mid-afternoon Monday and pulled her weekend bag out of the closet to start packing.

Sylvie called first. 'You're going to Santa Fe? Oh my God, how fabulous! Why is it that, when I have to travel out of town on business, it's a reading in Newark or a demo job in Poughkeepsie, but you get to go to Santa Fe?'

'Just lucky I guess,' Mac said, holding the phone to her ear with her shoulder.

'It's supposed to be just beautiful. Now you will tell me all about it as soon as you get back, right?' Sylvie said.

'Of course. But I don't think there'll be much to tell. We're only there a little over a day.'

'And you will let me know if there really are those Marlboro men cowboy types out there?' Sylvie whispered loudly into the phone. Mac knew she was still at her temp job of the week. Another receptionist position this time.

'Marlboro men? Sylvie, I think those are just an advertiser's dream.'

'And mine, honey. And mine. Oops, there's the big guy's line. Gotta go.'

When the phone rang again before she'd even walked away, Mac was sure it would be Sylvie again. But this was her professional line ringing, and it was Buratti on the other end.

'Mac, glad I caught you. Got a couple of things for you.'

Mac sat on the edge of her desk and pulled a notepad toward her. 'Okay, shoot.'

'I told you I'd check on Howard's little gambling problem. Well, a friend of mine from the old neighborhood – actually, I grew up with the guy – he has some ties to this particular organization we're talking about, let's say.'

'Okay, let's say that.'

'It seems Howard did have a little gambling problem, but not the usual kind. It wasn't like he was uncontrollable or anything. Just that he had the worst luck my guy has ever seen. Howard was the kind of player, from the way he tells it, if Notre Dame was playing Vassar, and Howard bet on Notre Dame, it was almost a sure bet that Vassar was gonna win.'

'Ooh,' Mac said, '*baad* luck.'

'Yeah, really bad luck,' Buratti continued. 'Anyway, they had nothing to do with him dying. They're pretty torn up about it as a matter of fact. The Atlantic City boys have been feeling the heat of the Indian gambling up in Connecticut, and losing a good customer like Howard – especially a good customer with rotten luck – puts a hole in their profits.'

'Well, Chad will be relieved that he doesn't have a gang of bookies after him, anyway.'

'Another thing. I heard from Jarvi today. He's been checking on His Lordship – this Boleigh guy. Seems he has been buying pretty heavy in New York and Boston in the last year or so. From what Jarvi heard, the guy has always been a player, but he's really been into it lately. We'll find out what we can and let you know.'

'Thanks, Mario. This is going to add up to dinner on me, or maybe on Chad, at the restaurant of your choice. Once you're through with Weight Watchers, of course.'

'Which is gonna be later rather than sooner, given the meal I put away at Minetta Tavern. But it was worth every bite.'

Mac met Chad at JFK the next morning at 6:30. Given when they'd had to get up in order to be at the airport on time, there was a minimum of chatting and both fell asleep as soon as they took off.

Like most New Yorkers, Mac considered herself well traveled since she'd been to Europe a few times. And like most easterners, she felt that she'd seen quite a bit of the United States because she knew the eastern seaboard rather well from Boston to Virginia, and she had visited Chicago and Los Angeles. Her opinions started to change when they flew down the spine of the southern Rockies toward Albuquerque.

By the time she and Chad were well into the drive from Albuquerque to Santa Fe, she was glad that Chad had won the toss over who was going to drive. She'd never seen views like this, where the vista was limited only by the curvature of the earth.

The beauty of the desert was so drastically different from the kind of natural beauty she was accustomed to, Mac found it hard to believe she was on the same planet, much less on the same continent or in the same country. By the time she saw the first signs for Santa Fe, Mac was regretting that the drive was only an hour and a half, and regretting that their

121

stay was less than forty-eight hours. She would have to come back.

They had arrived in Albuquerque to a crystal-clear day, heading toward seventy degrees, or so the woman at the car-rental desk had said. A storm had come through the day before, so they'd see snow on top of the mountains, she'd said, and she warned them it would be a little cooler in Santa Fe.

It was. But anybody who'd come out of New York, where the forecast was forty-two degrees and drizzle, wasn't about to complain over the sixty-two and sunny they found in Santa Fe.

The hotel Chad's travel agent had booked them in was unfortunately not one that echoed the adobe design of much of downtown Santa Fe. Rather, it was a cookie-cutter design, one of those hotel rooms that gave no clue as to what country you were in until you picked up the room-service menu.

They got settled in their adjoining rooms and Chad called Thomason Vandeveere, who invited them to come over within the hour. He gave Chad very good directions to get to his home, on one of the twisting roads that led up from the city. The drive there only gave Mac more reason to regret their stay would be so short.

Some people are lucky enough to be born with perfect pitch, and are said to have an ear. Thomason Vandeveere was born with an eye.

His mother, a proud sixth-generation Philadelphian and a serious student of the decorative arts, noticed that Tommy arranged his toys in an aesthetically pleasing manner from the time he was a toddler. He seemed to have an innate gift toward and appreciation for proportion and arrangement. By the time he was seven, he was racing through the Bible of fine American furniture, a reference book known in the trade as the 'Good, Better, Best' book because of the pictured comparative references to legs, finials, carvings, drawers, etc. Little Tommy started accompanying his mother to sales and auctions when he was ten and, walking through the pre-sale inspections, he'd point out pieces and whisper 'Better' to his mother, while pointing out a piece of furniture that matched the reference book's requirements. When he spotted a 'Best' and excitedly pointed it out to his mother, and she was able to buy the piece for an unexpectedly good price, she was convinced her boy had found his talent in life at an early age.

Little Tommy's talents didn't end with the study of furniture, however. In his early teens, classes at the Philadelphia Art Institute developed the eye he also had for painting and sculpture. He studied the market economics of the art world through his teens, and by the time he was eighteen and entering Columbia University's art-history program, Bartholomew's hired him as an intern. By the time he earned his bachelor's degree, which even his professors agreed was redundant, he was on full salary at the auction house. By the time he was twenty-five, he was heading their sales department.

Bartholomew's was smaller than its rivals Christie's and Sotheby's, but known to attract a smaller but somewhat more prestigious clientele. With only three offices – London, New York, and Hong Kong – Bartholomew's could not and did not compete with Christie's and Sotheby's on a world-market basis. But among the *crème de la crème* who owned and bought the *crème de la crème*, Bartholomew's was the house of choice.

Tom Vandeveere's appearance helped him enormously when he was first starting at Bartholomew's. He had a persistent squint to his face, which made him look like he had just smelled something offensive, or that he was looking over the shoulder of whichever person he was engaging in conversation. It was the perfect caricature of a snobbish look; it was the result, however, of ill-fitting contact lenses. When Vandeveere finally got properly fitting lenses, he kept up the squint consciously, because he found its fallout effects useful.

The other physical characteristic that contributed a great deal to Thomason Vandeveere's success in life was that he was six foot six. Most of the people in the art world had to crane their necks to talk to him. He could rather casually look down on them. It was a posture he found useful as well, especially on the days of important sales, when he 'addressed' the buying audience.

Mackenzie was startled when this giant of a man answered the door. She was accustomed to being around tall men. Chad, after all, was six-one, and Peter Rossellini was a little taller than Chad. But Thomason Vandeveere was quite a bit taller than they were, and a full foot taller than she was, which she found disconcerting. He was good-looking; even-featured with a broad, strong chin, he had a reddish blond cast to his hair, and gray eyes bordered by crow's feet that were more advanced than they should be for the age he was.

Chad had told her on the plane that Thomason Vandeveere was only thirty-five years old. He'd come very far in the art world very fast.

Vandeveere warmly welcomed them into his home. 'Good, you're here in plenty of time for the sunset,' he said. He ushered them through an entrance area to a large and beautiful living room. On the far side of the room were doors that opened onto a balcony, which offered a spectacular view to the south and west with not another house in sight. The golden afternoon sun streamed across the room, giving it a beautiful and clear warmth.

Vandeveere headed for the kitchen to get some 'sustenance' as he called it, and Chad followed behind him. Vandeveere apologized that he hadn't been more of a help on 'that odd belt reference'. 'Did you ever find out what it is – or was?' Mac heard him ask. She didn't have to listen for the answer.

Instead, she started looking around the room carefully. Mac was familiar with southwestern design, of course. Anybody who'd been around a decorating magazine or some of the trendier shops in Manhattan in the last ten years was accustomed to it, if not a little sick of it. But she'd never seen it in its natural habitat before, and that made all the difference in the world.

The neutral color of the walls and of most of the furniture drew attention to the color that was in the room: two medium-sized paintings that looked, to Mac's eye, to be southwestern primitives; a beautiful fabric wall hanging; and some vibrantly colored pillows piled on one end of the cream-colored sofa. As Mac surveyed the room she saw other touches here and there that indicated the presence of an art collector. Small bronze pieces drew the eye once you spotted them; three sat together on a table at the far end of the sofa. A two-and-a-half-foot wooden sculpture sat on the right wall, in between the two windows that faced the mountain.

Glancing around the room, seeing the way the outdoors and interior complemented each other, Mackenzie realized why this decor looked so much better here than she'd ever seen it before. An adobe wall set against the overcast northeastern sky looked drab, artificial and out of place. Adobe seen in the clear high desert air against the brilliant blue New Mexico sky looked and felt as comfortable as a cozy fire. Like the one in the corner Vandeveere was about to light.

'Isn't it a little warm for a fire?' Mac asked.

'This is your first visit to New Mexico, isn't it?' Vandeveere asked.

'Yes,' Mac replied cautiously to the apparent non-sequitur. She didn't see what that had to do with the temperature.

'You're about to observe a phenomenon of the high, dry desert. When the sun goes down, it's like somebody turns the heat off. But we'll wait a few minutes.'

Mac smiled politely, but decided she'd take what he was saying with a grain of salt. Then Chad walked in from the balcony, saying, 'Mac, you've got to come take a look at this view. But it's getting really chilly really fast. Bring your jacket.'

Out on the balcony, Vandeveere served the nachos he'd

made, and within a few minutes Mac understood his previous comment about the temperature drop. But the sunset was so beautiful she didn't want to risk looking away from the sky long enough to taste the nachos, even though she heard Chad raving about them. She'd never seen colors like this in the sky, not even in the best sunsets over the Sound, and she was fascinated with the way the reddish-gold of the sun played over the distant mesas and on the mountains to the right and to the left. It took her breath away, and she said so aloud.

As the sun winked behind the horizon, she realized Vandeveere was standing behind her left shoulder. 'It was pretty good,' he said. 'But not one of the great ones.' He looked down at her with a wink. 'A couple of us are talking about doing a rating system like they have in the Olympics. Then we could stand out on our balconies and hold up cards saying five point one, or five point eight or whatever. Of course, we'll need telescopes to see one another's scores. C'mon, let's get inside and light the fire. Chad, can you pick up the plate there?'

They settled between the couch and the armchair across from it, with the plate of nachos on the table in between. Vandeveere had the fire going within moments, and Mac had to admit it felt wonderful.

Chad scooped up another good-sized chip. 'I'll get out my pictures in a minute. But this is so good, I don't think I can resist. What in the world is in this cheese sauce?'

'Why don't we let the pictures wait until tomorrow morning?' Vandeveere said. 'Tonight's just for some talking and some of that *chile con queso* that you're enjoying. As long as you don't spoil your dinner, of course.'

127

Both Chad and Mac started to insist that they didn't expect dinner, since they certainly didn't want to put him to any trouble.

'Don't give it another thought,' he replied. 'It's almost all done. Anyway, it's a pleasure for me to be able to hear some of the gossip from back East instead of the Santa Fe gossip, believe me.' He sat back in the armchair and balanced his beer stein on the wide arm. 'So Karen tells me that Norman Jarvi also suggested you get in touch with me.'

'That's right,' said Chad. 'He thinks very highly of you, by the way.'

'Thanks,' Vandeveere said with a raise of his glass. 'It's always nice to hear. And the feeling's mutual. He asked for my help on a situation a few years back, I think it wasn't long after he started. Actually, it's one of the best scams I ever heard. This really bogus art-researcher type, very bullshit academic and very Park Avenue at the same time, starts approaching some minor private collectors. He did get his hand on some pretty nice pieces, however. Anyway, the collectors he approaches are all older women, whose taste in art he flatters shamelessly, and he asks their permission to borrow their painting, their whatever, for this research project he's doing.'

'What kind of research project was that?' Mac asked skeptically.

'This is the best. He tells them – and he has all these copies of magazine articles to prove it, which later Jarvi found out he'd created on his own PC with one of those desktop publishing programs – anyway, he tells them he's investigating the physiological response to aesthetic pieces.

He tells them that, once the research is published, this will be the way art's evaluated in the future, and if the painting they own was part of that original research, and is one of the items that generated the greatest physiological response – I don't know, maybe people were going to faint or something – that the value of their painting would shoot through the roof. So these nice ladies loan him these paintings, sculptures, what have you. They have official loan documents from the university, only it turns out to be a university no one's heard of before. Months go by, and the women don't hear from him, and it takes a while before it sinks in that they've been ripped off. When Jarvi got the first call, he thought the woman was a fool. By the time he found out about the fifth and sixth cases, that's when he came to me.'

'And what happened?' Mac asked.

'Fortunately, we were able to help him. They found the guy down in the Bahamas, and the ladies all got their art back except for one. Her treasure, alas, had disappeared into the great underworld of lost art.'

Chad stretched his arm along the back of the sofa, and leaned back, taking in the fire and the last fingers of light in the sky. 'This is a beautiful place. How long have you been here now?'

'Let's see. It was a year ago the first of June, so it's almost eighteen months.'

'Do you miss New York?' Mackenzie asked.

'Let me give you the long answer. When I first got out here, I did absolutely nothing for two, maybe three months.' Vandeveere took a healthy sip of his beer. 'Let me correct myself. I did nothing but learn how to put together a pretty damn good plate of nachos and I learned the joys of green chiles. That's chile with an "e" please, not chili with an "i" like those barbarians in Texas have. And then I waited for something to happen.'

'And?'

'And nothing did. Then I realized there was an essential difference between living in New York and living almost any place else. In New York, every day life runs over you like a steamroller and you respond or you go crazy or you die. But it's right there in your face every day. Here you have to go out and meet life. It's as busy as or as quiet as you want it to be.' He circled his finger around the top of the stein. 'It's different, that's for sure, but it's good right now. How long that will last, I don't know. But I'm here today and I'll be here tomorrow. And I've turned into one of the dreaded new Anglos of Santa Fe.'

'Anglo?' Chad said with a wrinkled forehead.

'In New Mexico, and throughout the southwest, I guess, if you're not Spanish or Hispanic, and you're not Indian, you're an Anglo. So the guy who opened this really good Jewish delicatessen, he's an Anglo. Another guy with an accent straight out of Naples, he's an Anglo. The Korean family that just moved in, they're Anglos. They probably consider blacks Anglos, for all I know. When I think what my Belgian grandfather, who *loathed* the British, would say if he heard his grandson described as an Anglo, it makes me laugh.'

'What was it that made you leave?' Mac asked.

'New York? Or Bartholomew's? Or both?'

'Both.'

'I've been doing what I do since I was a kid. And I got into this because I loved art, in whatever form. I loved the stories the Greek vases told me. I loved what an eighteenth-century desk told me about the way people lived. I loved the exuberance of Matisse, I loved what Bierstadt's paintings told me about nineteenth-century America. I've always felt a connection to the artist who's on the other side of this transaction. I always sensed that human connection. Like a hand stretching across time to tap you on the shoulder and say "I was here. This is how I lived. This is what I saw. This is what I did. This is what was important to me. This is what I thought of it." ' He took a long draught of his beer. 'Sort of a cosmic "Kilroy was here",' he added with a smile.

'And then, one day in the first week of June last year, when I realized that it had been almost ten years since I looked at anything without wondering primarily about its price, I decided it was time to stop – at least for a while.' He rimmed the edge of his beer stein with his index finger and it squeaked.

Chad nodded his understanding. ' "We must not lose sight of *ars gratia artis*", as Stephen Franklyn used to say. And probably still does.'

'Art for the sake of art, right?' Mac said. Her brother confirmed her translation. 'Mother would be thrilled to hear you spouting Latin, and appalled that you were quoting Stephen Franklyn.'

Chad leaned forward to grab the second-to-last nacho. 'Just because he's a jerk doesn't mean he isn't right once in a while.' He looked back over to Vandeveere. 'So that was it? You decided to bag New York and come out here?'

'It was one of those June days that let you know the summer in New York was going to be really sweaty,' Vandeveere replied. 'When you want to take a shower again by the time you get to your office in the morning. That only added to the speed of my decision.'

'So what depressed you more,' Chad asked, 'the excess humidity of the New York summers or the inflation in art prices in the last ten years?'

'Oh, the humidity wins by a long shot,' Vandeveere said quickly. 'The price of art never mattered to me, personally, one way or the other. Sure, our sales have set records, but so have all the other houses. It's the excitement of the auction that I love, and all of the work that goes into it before. A friend of mine in New York – a bit of a New Age waftie – put it well, I thought. It's not that money means anything *per se*, really, it's just the way we keep track.' He started to get up from his chair, and paused at the edge. 'If you don't mind the informality, why don't you join me in the kitchen while I finish dinner?'

Mac was impressed with the Spanish-tiled kitchen, which seemed absolutely enormous to her, given the kitchen she was accustomed to in New York. There was even room at the end of the large cooking island for a serving area, where she and Chad sat on high stools while Vandeveere whipped up what he described as his new favorite dish – boneless chicken breasts poached in white wine with sautéed mushrooms and artichoke hearts, served over pasta. If the smell was any indication, it could rapidly become one of Mac's favorite dishes, too.

132

Vandeveere shifted to sipping wine as soon as he started cooking. After he dumped a small bowl of sliced mushrooms into the frying pan, he picked up a wooden spoon and started stirring. And he picked up the conversation where it had left off in the living room.

'You know, the price of art is a curious thing,' he said, keeping the mushrooms moving in the pan. 'Art, if one accepts the broadest terms, makes the circle from Rembrandt and the masters of the Renaissance back to the cave paintings at Lascaux up to today's refrigerator art from some kid's kindergarten class. And in a way, money is what makes the difference. It's how we assign value. The cave paintings can't be bought because they can't be moved, like the Sistine Chapel, so we put them in a whole different category of priceless. And usually nobody fights over the price of refrigerator art, except in one *really* messy divorce case where I was called as an expert witness, if you can believe.

'What's interesting to me is that we don't assign this value necessarily by what these works mean to us personally. I suspect that refrigerator art is worth a lot more to parents out there than what they've got hanging on the wall in the living room. But we assign a value based on what somebody else might be willing to pay for it. Art acquires its value and its definition only when we sell it. Strange when you think about it, isn't it?'

In another frying pan, Vandeveere emptied a small bowl of halved artichoke hearts and poured a mixture of white wine, lemon juice and water over them to steam. He picked up his own wine glass with one hand and waved some of the cooking aroma toward him with the other.

Chad twirled the stem of his wine glass between his fingers. 'So what do you think of what's going on in the art world now? Have you kept up?'

'Not the way I would have if I were in New York, no. But some things you can see more clearly from a distance. One thing that started when I was still in New York I've been able to watch from here for the last year and a half. That's the situation with Russia and Germany and the whole Eastern European thing. It's been evident for a while that the floodgates opened, and nobody knows who or what's on first.' He walked toward the end of the island where they sat and leaned against the counter.

'I swear, when that statue of Lenin was being carted around Red Square or wherever, the half of the country that wasn't out demonstrating was back home in their grandma's attic digging out the souvenirs that grandpa brought back from World War II. I can't tell you the stuff that started showing up on the market three, four years ago.' A timer next to the stove chimed, and he returned to his pans. 'And God help us if the Hermitage keeps discovering these new "lost" collections. That could single-handedly rewrite the book on European art from 1750 to 1900.'

The dinner preparations were done within a few minutes, and Chad and Mac assisted in getting everything to the table. Vandeveere filled their wine glasses and as he was taking his seat he turned to Chad. 'I know we're not getting down to business until tomorrow,' he said as he made himself comfortable, 'but Karen told me something about your just having bought a gallery?'

Chad gave him a thumbnail sketch of the last two weeks,

hardly believing himself that it had actually been less than that since he'd signed the papers on River's End.

Vandeveere listened attentively, his eyes widening at appropriate points in Chad's narrative. 'And I'm assuming that dead bodies and getting beat up weren't part of your first-year business plan,' he said, as he served up a basket of rolls.

'Not exactly.'

After Mac's first few bites of the main course, she was convinced she'd found a new addition to her limited cooking repertoire. She murmured her praise to Vandeveere, and he executed a seated bow in thanks.

'Let me ask you this,' Mac said, steering the conversation to the subject that interested her. 'Don't worry, I'm not going to ask for the recipe – yet. But you don't seem to be much of a burned out-case, like you'd described before. Has this period of time away from the city, away from thinking of art only in terms of what its price is, has this been helpful to you?'

Vandeveere nodded. 'It has been, but I don't know just which element mattered most. Is it the fact that I've been eating regularly and getting plenty of rest? Or is it the fact that I don't ever have to deal with the Lexington Avenue line? Maybe it's the high desert air, or maybe it's taking the time to think and just listen to my own thoughts for a change.' He placed his fork on the side of the plate and sat back, reaching for his wine glass. 'But I can tell you that I had an extraordinary experience in September. I went to an exhibition here, at one of the local museums. There was a doll, I think it was two thousand, maybe twenty-two hundred

135

years old. Mesoamerican. Out of southern Mexico probably. Beautifully proportioned. A squat, rounded lower body,' he said, making the shape with his hands, 'a smaller upper body, and the head, tilted at *such* an angle!' The excitement he felt was evident in his voice, and it was thrilling to listen to him. 'The expression on the face was joyful, riveting. And for the first time in I don't know how long, I felt that hand reaching across the centuries, that human connection. It was like I could hear a voice saying, "See what I made for my child." And I swear to God, looking at this doll, you could hear a child's laughter.'

He picked up his wine glass and took a sip, because his throat was getting thick. Mac looked across the table at Chad, and she could tell he was as affected by Vandeveere's words as she was.

Vandeveere cleared his throat and set down his glass. 'So I guess you could say it's been helpful.'

EIGHT

Given the time change and their travel, Chad and Mac were exhausted by the time they returned to the hotel at nine. They were due back at Vandeveere's house, with pictures, in twelve hours.

They met down in the coffee shop at seven-forty-five, after Mac had strolled through downtown Santa Fe for over a half-hour, giving herself more reason to return in the near future. By eight-fifteen, Mac knew she had just enough time to get to her room, change clothes, and do something in the way of make-up before they left for Vandeveere's house again.

Vandeveere greeted them with more coffee, hot and strong, and then it was down to business pretty quickly. They sat at his large dining table, after Mac once again admired the astonishing views out to the mountains and down onto the mesas. It was just as beautiful in full morning light.

Chad had kept the pictures grouped as the materials had been when they found them, and Vandeveere looked at them that way. Chad showed him the photos of the group of six paintings first, and Vandeveere studied them virtually without comment. Then he studied the pictures of the Greek and Roman pieces, arranging them carefully in front of him on the table. He left them in place as he studied the third batch of pictures, the one containing the mixture of items.

After quizzing Chad some on details, he moved to the side and took a good swig of coffee. 'You're right, of course,' he said to Chad, 'I can't tell you anything about the authenticity just by looking at the pictures. Especially with the pots and the sculptures. A friend of mine out here says you have to "hold them, smell them, feel the spirits". I think he's right in a way. The sculptures, the pitchers, the jars, these aren't just static pieces of art, these mean something in people's everyday lives. Or meant something. And I think that meaning accumulates.' He put his mug down to refill it again, then glanced back at Chad. 'Assuming they're authentic, of course.'

'Tom, do you have any idea what Malcolm Howard would be doing with this collection of things?'

'Except for the paintings, no. I knew that he had this small gallery up in Registon, and that he did some business in the American impressionists and some nineteenth-century American. But, as I said, I didn't know the man well at all.' He fingered a few of the pictures by the edges, moving them slightly on the table. 'What really intrigues me is this collection of Greek and Roman.'

'Why is that?' Mac said just before Chad could.

'I know a couple of guys – middlemen you'd call them. They're dealers but not the kind of dealer who has a store or a gallery—'

'Are we talking the kind of dealer who deals out of the trunk of a car?' Mac asked.

Vandeveere laughed easily. 'No, it's not quite that bad. These fellows just work a bit more casually than most. At any rate, they started buying up what Greek and Roman pieces came on the market in the late eighties. There were a number of people, these guys included, who thought there would be a real resurgence of interest in this kind of antiquity as we got into the nineties. There've been revivals before, especially in the late nineteenth century, but even before that, during the Renaissance.' He reached for one of the Polaroids and propped it on the bottom edge so it stood upright for a moment. 'When big milestones are coming up, like the turn of the century, not to mention the turn of the millennium, there has been a tendency for society to turn its attention to the ancient world, and or to the spiritual world. Some people think this whole New Age thing, not to mention the rise in fundamentalism of all kinds, is an end-of-the-century or end-of-the-millennium phenomenon.'

Vandeveere leaned back in his chair, lengthening his spine. 'You know, in the tenth century, people were properly cowed by the millennium. Thought it was the end for sure. It's almost sad that our biggest contest is going to be which car company – and where it will be from, Detroit or Tokyo – is going to be the first to come up with the model 2000 something. The millennium has turned into a marketing opportunity. Sad.'

He leaned over the table again, attention back on the photos. 'Be that as it may, these guys are still around, and if Howard or anybody was buying or dealing on this level they should know about it. I can try to get in touch and let you know over the weekend.'

139

'That would be great,' Chad said.

Vandeveere sat back down at the table. 'I don't know what to make of a few of these things.' He moved the photograph of the leather-bound manuscript in front of him, and then the photo of the gargoyle that had scared Mac back in the storage room in New London. 'Tell me about these again.'

'The manuscript is of the Gospels. There's a dedication page with the year 1402. The dedication page is quite beautiful, and the beginning pages of each of the Gospels appear to have the name of the writer of that Gospel – Matthew, Mark and so forth, in large gold letters.'

'What's its condition?'

'It looked fairly good to me for a book that's almost six hundred years old, but I have absolutely no experience with manuscripts.'

'Much color in the illuminations?'

'On the dedication page, yes. Even Mac noticed the lapis color. Gold on the first pages of the Gospels, like I said. Large red letters at the beginning of sections, smaller red letters at the chapter breaks. Why?'

Vandeveere put the picture down on the table again and looked over at Chad. 'This is an odd thing for anybody to forge. Hard to imagine the time and effort it would take. If it's for real, and depending on its condition, you could have a fortune sitting right there.'

'Like what?' Chad asked, surprised.

'About ten years ago, maybe a little more, an illuminated manuscript of the Gospels sold for about twelve million.'

'Twelve million *dollars*?' Mac asked, astonished.

Vandeveere nodded at her with a smile. 'Now, I don't think you're in that league. That one had a lot of historical context to it, as I recall, and the illuminations were extraordinary. It sounds like the one you have was a little more everyday at the monastery, if you know what I mean. But if the date can be verified, you've got something there.

'As to this,' he said, picking up the photo of the gargoyle, 'you have any idea what it is, having looked at it, held it?'

'Specifically, no,' Chad said. 'It's obviously weathered, but it's hard to tell if that's thirty winters' wear or three hundred. As to what it came off of, your guess is as good as mine.'

'I suggested maybe it was a medieval scarecrow,' Mackenzie offered, 'because it certainly scared me when I looked at it.'

'Can I keep this picture?' Vandeveere asked Chad. 'I'll only need it for a few days, and then I can get it back to you.'

'Sure,' Chad agreed. 'On the manuscript. Any ideas who I can go to to check it out?'

'Yes. I'm going to give you a few names and numbers before you leave. And I'll make some calls while you're here, too.'

'Thanks,' Chad said. 'That'll be a real help. What do you think I should do about authenticating these antiquities?'

'Without the resources of a museum, that's going to be a tough one,' Vandeveere said, pointing to two of the pictures. 'Ancient sculpture is hard to test. Marble is marble, the stone is as old as it is. What you have to try to figure out is the age of the hammer blows that turn the stone into art. There are some sophisticated tests, but a bit expensive. And if you have dolomitic marble versus calcitic marble, the tests are different, so that has to be determined as well.'

Mac leaned forward in her chair. 'Tell me, do museums or collectors have to go through these kinds of tests with every purchase?'

'Oh, no,' Vandeveere said. 'Usually there's a provenance and, in the case of pieces like this, that provenance would hopefully state where it was discovered, or where it was first traded, something like that. In cases like that, your expert will rely on the style of the piece, its iconography, if the history of the piece and its appearance gives it some context, and if it all makes sense they proceed on that basis.'

'How about the pottery?' Chad asked.

'Authenticating it, you mean?' Chad nodded yes.

'Actually, there's a very good process for authenticating ceramics and terra cotta. It's called thermoluminescence analysis.' Vandeveere saw Chad's eyes widen, and Mac's looked like they were going to glaze over. 'Trust me. It's not as bad as it sounds. From what I gather, this process measures the electrons in the material, in the clay itself. Apparently all those electrons are wiped out when a piece is fired, but from the moment it's taken out of the fire or the kiln it starts building up electrons again. So when these pieces are heated in the right way by people who know what they're doing and who won't melt them or explode them, they give off a glow. The new electrons, you see? They create the thermoluminescence. So these people who know what they're doing measure that thermoluminescence and they can age those pieces pretty specifically.'

'That's amazing,' Mac said.

'It is. But actually, the most interesting area I've read about lately is archaeometry.'

'What's that?' Chad asked.

'People from all different parts of the art world and scientific community. You've got art historians, restorers, archaeologists, physicists, chemists, geologists, and God know who else involved in this.'

'And just what is it that they're involved in?'

'Through this kind of interdisciplinary back-and-forth, these archaeometrists can tell if a piece of sculpture, or even a bronze – by the way, this might help you with some of these bronzes – they can tell if it was worked with tools that didn't exist at the time the piece was supposedly created.'

Mac had been listening attentively. 'If I'm not mistaken, it sounds like these tests are meant to invalidate the works rather than authenticate them, am I right?'

Chad interrupted before Vandeveere could answer. 'I think it's like what Detective Jarvi said to us. It's easier to prove that something is a fake than it is to prove that it's genuine.'

'Absolutely right. And these tests have proved a lot more successful than many in the art world would care to know. I read an article on one European scientist – I can't remember if he's a chemist or physicist, but he's the co-developer of one of these new tests they're using. He said that half the stuff he's examined in the last ten years, and that comes to thousands of pieces, fully half of them are fake. But he knows that, even after the tests, they're still sitting there in the museums around the world.'

'This is astonishing to me,' Mac said. 'I feel like a babe

in the woods. Do you mean that some of the things I've admired at the Metropolitan could be fakes?'

'Sure. They had a couple of big pieces they had to remove from the collection when it became public that they were fakes, but that goes back a few years.'

Vandeveere was obviously enjoying the discussion, and he got up to replenish everyone's coffee with the last of the pot.

'But there are all sorts of creative fakes out there. For the phony Greek statues, these guys get a reasonably competent sculptor to re-create a piece that's sort of a combination of a few, then they whack a piece off the nose, chip the ear and the eyebrow a bit, bury it in cow manure, or apply some acids, and *presto chango* you've got a statue that looks like it's weathered twenty-five hundred Mediterranean winters.' He laughed when he saw Mackenzie's expression. It was the cow manure that had taken her aback.

'Two things I'm going to do for you,' Vandeveere continued. 'No, make that three, because I already said I'd put together the names and numbers for you. Next, I'm going to make a call so you can get into a sale at Bartholomew's on Friday. You're flying back tomorrow morning, right?'

'Right,' said Chad. 'What's the sale and why should we be going?'

'It's a private collection from Boston. Bradford is the name, and it's going to be a big, big sale. I was in on the early discussion almost two years ago, so that's how I know about it. The range of interests is as catholic – with a small "c" – as the collection you've got here,' he said, gesturing to the photos still spread across the table. 'Maybe more so. I know there are American impressionists included, some particularly good seascapes as I remember, some Greek vases, one or two Hudson River paintings, lots of stuff. The collector was an old man, too, and he stopped acquiring years ago, so this stuff has been off the market for thirty, maybe forty years. That usually brings them out of the woodwork. If Howard was fronting for a group of collectors, or a collector, they'll probably be represented at the sale. A friend of mine from Philadelphia will probably be there, and I'll ask him to hook up with you.

'Second thing – no, it's the third thing, isn't it?' Vandeveere continued. 'I'm going to make a call to a friend in New Jersey. An acquaintance actually. Angelo Campanelli's an interesting type, He's sort of a talent agent for forgers. These major pieces – the manuscript, the fifteenth-century Venetian piece – if they're fakes, and if they've been done here in the last twenty years, he'll know about them. I don't think he'll be as much help on the Greek, but you never know.

'Let me add a fourth thing,' he said, standing up from the table. 'I'm going to go make us lunch.'

They left his place mid-afternoon, after Vandeveere had placed some of the calls he'd promised to. Chad was leaving with a handful of notes on who to contact and how. He also hoped he was leaving with the beginnings of a new friendship. Vandeveere had been an enormous help, and Chad told him so.

Sonny was almost through searching Griffin's room. He had to admit the guy was pretty neat – for a guy, that is. He

145

moved toward the connecting door to see how Buster was doing. He'd gotten suspicious when Buster had insisted on seaching the sister's room. He was just weird enough to be puttin' her underpants on his head or something worse.

God, he wished this job were over. The last couple of weeks working with Buster had been even worse than the couple of months before. Even this trip to New Mexico. It would have been exciting at another time. He'd never been west of Philadelphia before, and he'd loved westerns as a kid. Some of that scenery on the drive up here looked straight out of those old Clint Eastwood movies, even though he'd heard those were made in Italy or Spain or someplace else non-American. Anyway, there was no chance for western sightseeing this time. This was one hurry-up and move trip, and now that they weren't finding anything he'd have to check in with the old man again, and they'd probably be back on the plane tonight.

This trip had been a long shot anyway, and he figured they were here only because the cops were still keeping the gallery under watch and the old man wanted them doing *something*. Even though no one had asked for his opinion lately, Sonny figured that neither of these Griffins knew shit about the belt.

He sucked in his breath and headed for the door to get Buster. Buster had been even more obnoxious than usual since they flew out of Providence, which Sonny would have thought was impossible. But he'd started on the plane, with the remarks to the stewardesses that Sonny thought were going to get them thrown out at 35, 000 feet. Then he insisted on driving once they got to the Albuquerque airport, claiming that, since neither one of them had ever been here before, it didn't make any difference who drove. Of course, that didn't take into consideration that he, Sonny, actually read road signs and didn't just follow his goddam nose when he was driving. Then, around noon, as they're pulling off the exit into Santa Fe, they came to a red light at the end of the ramp and in the left lane there's a pick-up truck with three Indians in the front seat. Buster taps on his horn, rolls down the window and gives them the finger, saying 'Hey, Kemo Sabe, you lost!!' and laughing like it was a joke. Watching the expression in the Indians' eyes, for about a minute there Sonny was as scared as he's been since high school, but then Buster squealed away from the corner into his right turn and the pick-up didn't follow them.

Then when they finally got to the hotel and found out the rooms, instead of letting Sonny pick the locks, which, okay, he wasn't great at, but pretty good, Buster had insisted on stealing the master keys from the cleaning woman's cart. Sonny tried to point out how that was more dangerous, but it was like talkin' to a wall. What with casin' out the floors, double-checking the room numbers and getting the key, it was three o'clock before they got into the rooms. And it was comin' up on three-thirty now and they had *nothin'*.

'Come on, let's get out of here,' Sonny said quietly as he stepped into the other room. Buster was bent over the dresser-type thing and shoved the drawer shut fast. Of course, it was an empty drawer because this asshole had dumped everything onto the bed. *Very smart*, Sonny wanted to say. *Very smart. Somebody'd have to be in this room two, three seconds before they knew it'd been tossed. Shit.* With a

147

jerk of his head he motioned for Buster to get out into the hall.

They'd stashed the keys back in the laundry cart as soon as they'd gotten the doors open, so they headed for the elevator they'd come up on. They waited and waited, until it became apparent that only one out of the two elevators was in service. Sonny pressed his ear against the door. It sounded like it was all the way down in the lobby. Shit, it was only four flights down. 'Come on,' he said to Buster. 'Let's take the stairs.'

Chad and Mac were planning on a quiet dinner, and a light one, given the size of the lunch Tom had fixed. It would also have to be an early one, since they would once again be leaving well before dawn to make their plane back to New York.

They'd already been waiting a few minutes for the elevator, since only one of the two cars was in service. Mac heard somebody coming down the stairwell. She was debating about taking the stairs up – it was only four flights, after all – but before she could mention the idea to Chad the elevator door opened. She stepped into the empty car and headed for the back wall. As soon as she took a breath, she turned to Chad.

'Do you smell that?'

He tested the air with a few sniffs. 'Yeah,' he said tentatively.

'That's the same scent as that guy who jumped me in the elevator wore.'

'So?'

'So I'm saying that I think the guy who jumped me at the school was in this elevator.'

'Mackenzie, I think every drugstore in the country sells it. Not to mention every K-Mart and Wal-Mart, too. I don't think we can call the cops because somebody's wearing cologne.'

'It's not that they're wearing cologne,' Mac said, annoyed with her brother. 'It's the degree to which they're wearing it.'

'Are you sure you're just not letting the aroma and the fact that you're in an elevator run away with you?'

'Chadwick, it's not like this is only the second elevator I've been in in my life,' Mac replied briskly. Chad could tell she was a little pissed because she'd used his full name.

As they walked down the hall to their rooms, Mac told him she was planning on making a few calls and then maybe getting out to walk again. There seemed to be plenty of time, since they still had a few hours even before an early dinner. They agreed to knock on each other's door around six-thirty.

Mac unlocked her door first, and Chad was opening his when he heard her. 'Dammit all to hell!' Mackenzie said, loudly.

'What?!' Chad said, almost dropping his key at hearing his sister swear like that. 'What's the matter?' He followed her through the still-open door. Mackenzie's room was a mess. Her suitcase had been up-ended, every drawer had apparently been emptied onto her bed. And from the looks of the pillows, even the bed had been pulled apart.

Mackenzie stepped to the bathroom door and flipped on the light. Her make-up case and toiletries had been gone

149

through as well. 'Ooh, this gives me such a case of the creeps. Those gonzos going through my underwear? Ugh.' She shivered.

'Let me check next door,' Chad said. 'I'm going to find the same thing there, I'm sure. Then we'll call hotel security.'

Chad's room had been searched, but it didn't look as bad. A few of the clothes he'd hung up sat rumpled on the floor of the closet area, the pillows on the bed had been pulled out and then replaced, and the drawers gone through, but rather neatly.

The hotel security officer was a retired Albuquerque cop who didn't need this kind of hassle. It was almost a half-hour by the time he got the chart from housekeeping that showed when the rooms had been cleaned. Their rooms had been among the first done on this floor, and the maid signed them done by 9:45. Since they hadn't returned until after three-thirty, that left a window of almost six hours in which whoever it was could have come and gone.

'We had a thing this afternoon where a maid thought she'd lost her keys, but we found them in the bottom of the laundry cart, so I don't think that was anything,' the security guy assured them. 'How long will it take you to go through and tell me what's missing?'

'I've already looked through my belongings. Nothing's missing,' Mac said.

Chad said the same. The security guy looked at them with a squint to one eye. 'You don't seem to be surprised at this.'

'No, unfortunately,' Mackenzie said. 'We're not. They're looking for something we don't have. We'd appreciate it if you would report it to the police, however. We may need the report at some point in the future.'

'Okay,' he said reluctantly. 'But the manager's gonna be mad about this. It's not like it's a theft or anything. Looks bad on the corporate record, you know.'

'I'm sorry, but I'll have to insist that you make a police report,' Mac said, walking him to the door. 'Thank you.'

Chad was still mad enough to throw things when he got back into his own room. It hadn't been more than two minutes since the security officer had left when there was a knock at the door. Chad figured the guy was back, trying to worm his way out of making the police report behind Mac's back. Chad pulled the door open with a yank. 'What?' he said, loudly, and then he noticed it wasn't the security guy at all.

It was a beautiful young woman with dark red hair and troubled brown eyes. She was dressed in jeans and a denim workshirt and looked absolutely fabulous in them.

'Chad? Chad Griffin?' she said, nervously biting her lip as she finished.

He had absolutely no idea who she was. 'Yes?'

'I guess you don't remember me. I'm Elizabeth – Beth – de Beaupre. I was a freshman at Riverside when you were a senior. Art-history department.'

Chad stared at her intently, and some faint twinge of recognition stirred. It was going back about eight years. 'Yes, of course,' he said, trying to sound pleasant. The last thing he needed right now was a school reunion.

'I heard you bought Malcolm Howard's gallery.'

'Yes,' Chad said, slowly. Buying a gallery in a small town

151

in Connecticut wasn't the kind of news that made it across the continent this fast.

'And I heard you might be looking into what happened to Mr Howard.'

'Yes,' he said again, even more on alert than he was before.

She looked down at her feet, and then up again at him, and Chad saw tears shining on the rims of her eyes. 'I think I need your help. I think maybe somebody's going to try and kill me.'

NINE

Chad took Beth de Beaupre's hand and guided her into the room. He got her seated at the little table by the window and, because she looked like she needed it, keyed open the mini-bar to get her a brandy.

He pounded on the connecting door to Mackenzie's room and, *sotto voce*, repeated Beth's words at the door. Mackenzie peeked around the door, nodded, and said she'd be right in as soon as she finished changing.

When Mac entered, Chad made the introductions, and Mackenzie took the other chair at the table. Chad sat on the bed, wishing he could pull it closer.

'Beth, why don't you tell us what you have to do with all of this. Why do you think somebody might be out to kill you?' he asked softly.

The young woman had managed to hold off her tears, but it was obvious she was extremely nervous. The fresh tissue Chad had given her was almost dust, but she continued to wring it through her hands. 'I'm not sure where to start. It goes back a couple of years, I guess. The guy who turned me onto this – you might remember him, Chad, he was the year ahead of me at Riverside. Randy Toffmeyer.'

Chad nodded. 'I remember the name. I'm sure I'd recognize him if I saw a picture.'

'I'd been out of graduate school for almost two years when I ran into Randy. I was in a nowhere job with a library collection up in Boston, and Randy was working at the Seattle Museum. Anyway, he told me there might be this opportunity working for Mr Howard. Not working for him directly, like at the gallery or anything. It was more like he'd help you get a really good job. Randy said he had contacts in cities around the country. He'd just be wanting you to keep your eyes open for something for him.'

'To steal?' Mac asked.

Beth looked at her, wide-eyed. 'No, I don't think so. That's not the impression I had. It was more of letting him know what came up on the market, what the museum might be trying to acquire, that kind of thing.' She took a sip of the brandy from the water glass Chad had given her. 'Anyway, I told Mr Howard that I'd be interested in relocating to the southwest, particularly Santa Fe, but I knew that it would be impossible to come here without a job. Six months later, he contacts me and says there's an opening here at the Museum of the Southwest, and would I be interested. Would I ever, I said, but I didn't think I had the resumé to get the interview. Mr Howard told me to send the resumé to him, and within ten days I got the call to come down for the interview.' She sipped the brandy again and paused.

'And?' Chad urged her on.

'And I got the job. Mr Howard wrote to congratulate me and all, but I didn't hear from him again until about a year later. It was in mid-June of this year. He said there was a particular piece he was looking for that might be coming on the market and to let him know the minute I heard anything. "The belt" he called it, and he really wanted to acquire it. He made it sound like a matter of life and death.'

Chad and Mac looked at one another, wide-eyed. Chad turned back to Beth. 'What else do you know about the belt, Beth? Anything?'

'No. I had no idea what he was talking about and I asked as many questions as I could without giving myself away, but no.' She paused and looked directly at Mac. 'He was very secretive about it, using code words, like he was playing spy.'

'Did you hear anything around the museum in the last six months about a belt?' Mackenzie asked.

'No, nothing.'

'Still, this doesn't explain why you think somebody might be about to kill you, Beth. What haven't you told us?' Mac asked as gently as she could.

'Last spring, before I heard from Mr Howard, I ran into Randy Toffmeyer again. He was at a meeting of museum personnel up in Denver. We talked for a while, he talked about what a great deal this was with Mr Howard, how he'd turned him onto another guy from Riverside, Paul Noble from the class behind me, and how Paul had gotten a job at a museum in Tulsa because of Mr Howard. It turned out Paul was at the meeting, too, and I got to see him the next day. We talked a little bit, because our museums have pretty similar collections. When I saw Randy just before he left Denver, he was all excited because he'd just talked to Mr

Howard and he thought he was about to steer him onto something big. The next I heard of Randy, one of my old room-mates who lives in Tacoma calls me and says that she just read Randy Toffmeyer's death notice in the paper.'

Chad looked at his sister, then at Beth. 'When was this?'

Beth looked down, concentrated. 'Late June or early July. I know it was after I talked to Mr Howard.'

'What was the cause of death?'

'Hit-and-run accident. Another car hit his and the gas tank exploded. He never made it out of the car.' She reached for the glass and swallowed the last of the brandy.

'There's more to this story, isn't there?' Mac said. Beth nodded yes. 'Chad, why don't you get her another brandy?' Beth started to demur, then changed her mind.

Chad got the other small bottle from the mini-bar and cracked the seal open. 'There's a wine glass in there, too, Chad,' his sister said. 'Why don't you get that for her?'

With the typical younger brother smile, he did as she suggested, then cleared away the water glass and the empty bottle before taking his seat again on the bed.

'Okay?' Mac asked.

Beth nodded. 'Two weeks ago, Mr Howard called me.' She frowned and stared up at the ceiling for a moment. 'Yes, it was just two weeks ago tonight, because it was the night before Halloween. He called late at night, at home, which was strange, because it's two hours difference between here and the east coast. He said a contact in Oklahoma had been able to acquire the belt for him, so that I needn't keep an eye out for him any longer. He said he probably wouldn't be bothering me again in the future, and I told him it was

certainly no bother. Then I told him how sorry I was to hear
about Randy, and he asked what I was talking about. He
hadn't heard about Randy dying, which surprised me. He
was pretty upset when we got off the phone.' She swirled the
fresh brandy around in her glass and lifted the glass to sniff
the aroma. The wine glass was much better than the water
glass. 'In the next day or so I got to thinking that it must have
been Paul who scored this belt thing for Mr Howard, and I
was still curious about what it was. But you know how you
think to call somebody, but whenever you're thinking to call,
you're in the shower or something. So it wasn't until this past
Monday that I called the museum in Tulsa. When I asked for
Paul, the woman started hemming and hawing.'

'Paul's dead, too?' Chad asked, astonished.

Beth nodded yes.

'Let me guess,' Mac said. 'A hit and run.'

Beth nodded again. 'On Halloween. He was going to meet
some friends from the museum at a costume party. He was
dressed like Zorro, the woman said. She said the police
figured it was probably a drunk driver who panicked and left
the scene.'

'How did you find out about Malcolm Howard?' Mac
asked.

Beth rolled her eyes. 'That I just found out today.
Somebody heard through the art grapevine out here that you'
– she indicated Chad with a dip of her head – 'were here to
see the guy from Bartholomew's.'

'Word does get around pretty quick, doesn't it?' Chad
said.

'Anyway, I called one of my classmates who's working

157

up in Hartford to see if she knew why you'd be coming to see him.' Beth blushed a little in the telling of this part of the story. 'And she's the one who told me about Mr Howard. She said it was all over the news in Hartford.'

'Yes, it was,' Chad said.

'And she said you bought his gallery.'

'Yes, I did,' he said with a sheepish grin. Each day that went by, that was sounding like less and less of a sound business decision.

'I just freaked when I heard about him, especially after hearing about Paul two days ago. I don't know what's going on, but I'm scared.'

Mac rose, and put her hand on the younger woman's shoulder. 'I don't think you're foolish to be scared, but I don't know if there's real reason to suspect that they might be after you as well. It appears like you were involved in Mr Howard's business only tangentially. Those people who are dead seem to have been directly involved.' She turned to her brother. 'I'm going to go call Buratti, see if he'll make some calls to Seattle and Tulsa tomorrow.'

'Now?' Chad said, looking at his watch. 'It'll be close to seven in New York, won't it?'

'I have his home number. And if I don't reach him tonight, I can call when we get to the airport in the morning.' She turned back to Beth. 'Let me get you a piece of paper, Beth,' she said, and found the guest pad on the desk/dresser combination. 'Please write down the names of the two men you told us about. The last one I know you said died on Halloween, but please give me an approximate date of death for the man from Seattle.'

Beth wrote out the information requested and handed Mac the whole pad.

'I'll tap on the door when I'm off the phone,' Mac said, and disappeared into her own room.

'So,' Chad started, 'I'm tempted to say "how've you been", except it sounds like that bad old joke – "other than that, Mrs Lincoln, how did you like the play?" '

Beth gave him a weak smile and swirled her brandy again before taking another sip. 'You know, Chad, it wasn't just because of all this that I called my friend in Hartford.'

'No?' he said.

'No,' Beth said. 'I hadn't heard anything about you in a few years. You were in Washington a few years ago; that was the last I read in the Art Alumni notes.'

'Well, that was true up until about two and half weeks ago, so I guess you didn't miss out on much news.'

'But still, I was thrilled when I heard you were in Santa Fe,' she said with a shy smile.

'Thrilled? That seems a little extreme.'

She looked down into the glass. 'It must be the brandy talking. Normally, I'd never have the guts to say this. But I always had a crush on you back at Riverside. I know you were a big senior guy, not about to notice a lowly freshman like me. But those differences sort of evaporate, don't they? A couple of years' difference doesn't matter.'

Now it was Chad's turn to blush. 'No, they don't seem to matter. But—'

'You're embarrassed that I have a crush on you?' she interrupted.

'No, it's very flattering, Beth, but—'

159

'Oh, my God, you're married, aren't you? Or engaged? Which is it?' She didn't give him time to answer. 'It's the brandy talking. Like I said, I never would've had the guts to bring this up.' She raised a hand to her forehead, as though to shield her eyes, then peeked out from under it. 'You're married. That's it, isn't it?'

'No, Beth, I'm not married. I'm gay.'

Her hand dropped into her lap, dead. 'What?' she said in a flat voice.

'I'm sorry. I'm gay. I mean I'm not sorry I'm gay, but – oh, you know what I mean.'

She leaned an elbow on the table then caught her head in her hand. 'I do not like the way my life is going,' she said, not particularly to Chad. 'I have the first good job I've ever had, I'm finally able to pay more than the minimum on my credit cards, only there's this *teeny* problem that someone might be trying to kill me. With my luck, they're probably drug smugglers or something. I finally find the guy I've had a crush on since I was eighteen and he turns out to be gay.' She looked at Chad, as if suddenly remembering his presence. 'Not that there's anything wrong with gay people, you understand.'

Chad nodded. 'It's just that you wish I weren't one of them. Like I said, Beth, it's very flattering.'

Mac tapped on the door and Chad got up to open it. 'There are a couple of things I need to speak to you about,' Mac said, 'but first, why don't we order room service?'

'Have dinner in the room?' Chad said. 'I thought we were—'

Mackenzie shook her head to silence him. 'Let's take a

look at the menu and maybe Beth can call down while we go into my room for a minute.'

Chad grumbled only until he realized that the room-service menu looked quite good. Beth wrote out the order and was set to call it in when they stepped into Mac's room.

'Okay, what's going on?' Chad said.

'First, room service was Buratti's idea. He said if those guys have been in the hotel, which we know they have, even going down to the dining room is a bad idea. Second, he says we need to get her under wraps for a few days until we know it's safe. I don't think she should even go back to her home.'

'Where do you think she should go?'

'We'll figure that out over dinner.

'Third, Buratti says that if we were planning on leaving for the airport at five, we better leave at four. If these guys are keeping a watch on the hotel, leaving an hour early might throw them off.'

'Okay, four o'clock it is.'

'How is she doing?' Mackenzie asked.

Chad gave a half-hearted smile, and then told Mac of the conversation that had just transpired.

'Still breaking hearts, are you, Chadwick?' she said with a soft smile in return. It wasn't the first time this had happened. And probably it wouldn't be the last.

Chad's homosexuality had been discussed in their home just about as much as Mac and Whitney's heterosexuality had been, which is to say, never. Any sex education that occurred in their home, if that was even the applicable term, had been handled by Stella. It consisted of a few terse conversations, a run-down on basic biological functions, and, for the girls, a brief seminar on feminine sanitary products.

Mac remembered a stumbling conversation with Stella when she was about sixteen, when she tried to express her concern that Chad seemed more than usually vulnerable to the cruelties of mid-adolescence. Stella had patted her hand and assured her, 'Chadwick's a special lad, girl. He'll be fine.'

Mac and Chad were virtually adults, with Chad already in college, before they talked about it openly for the first time. The 1980s were not an easy time for a young gay man to come of age. Mackenzie often thought back to Stella's words. *He's a special lad. He'll be fine.* And he was.

The hotel decor might be cookie-cutter tacky, but the room-service menu was first rate. Mackenzie's room was the most put-back-together, so they ended up eating in there. Mac gingerly brought up the subject of the security at Beth's residence and, when she said she lived in a multi-unit apartment that sounded like it had no security whatsoever, they inquired if there was any place else she might stay.

She really didn't have any other options, since she didn't yet know that many people in town who had a better living arrangement than she did.

Mac suggested that Chad called Tom Vandeveere to see if he had any recommendations, and he went into his room to place the call. He didn't close the connecting door all the way, and within a few minutes Mac heard what she knew was Chad's cajoling tone of voice. Tom Vandeveere was being talked into something.

When Chad walked back in a few minutes later, he said to Beth, 'If you don't mind, he says you can stay with him.'

'With Thomason Vandeveere? Really?' Beth's eyes grew wide.

'I think it's a good idea, don't you, Mac? That place where he's staying is on a couple of acres up there, there's a security patrol on the road at night, he says. I think it's your best bet,' he said, looking at Beth. 'Hopefully, it will only be for a few days.'

Chad said he'd drive Beth to her apartment to pick up a few things, and then up to Vandeveere's house. Mac insisted on going with them, and even she didn't know if it was to add her protection to Chad's, or if she just didn't want to stay by herself at the hotel.

Tom Vandeveere's rigid-lipped smile on welcoming Beth to his home confirmed to Mac that Chad had verbally strong-armed the man somehow. They didn't linger long at Vandeveere's house after making those awkward introductions, and they were back at the hotel before nine. Normally that would seem like a nice early evening, Mac thought, but when you have to leave a wake-up call for three, it's suddenly very late.

The drive back down to the airport went by with little conversation, but with some good music, thanks to an all-night Albuquerque radio station they picked up once they were on the highway. Mac had also insisted they stop at the twenty-four-hour gas station *cum* coffee shop, where they loaded up on four large cups of coffee that was definitely not decaffeinated. One of Peter's songs came on the radio when they were a half-hour out of Santa Fe. It was one of Mac's favorites from a year ago, '*What Will It Take*'. When she reached over to turn up the volume, Chad didn't even tease her. She realized he must be very tired to miss such an opportunity.

They got to the airport at quarter past five, and had plenty of time before their flight. After they had a leisurely breakfast and traded a few newspapers between them, Chad still had to wait until a few minutes past seven before he could make the call he'd thought about last night.

He finally got through to the alumni office at Riverside University at seven-fifteen. Mac could see him gesturing toward the phone like he had a video connection with the office in Connecticut. After a few minutes, he came back to the boarding area where she was waiting.

'Well?'

'I think the woman's a lame-brain, but she's not as much of a lame-brain as I thought.'

'How so?'

'I said to her, didn't anybody notice that you have certain alumni – certain young alumni – showing up dead way ahead of the actuarial tables? Didn't you think to mention it to anybody?'

He sat down in the chair next to her. 'And she said she did. She reported it to the editor of the alumni news, and news of Toffmeyer's death will be in the fall edition, which is late getting out. She just got the word on Paul Noble last week, so his death notice will be in the winter edition. The only other person she told was the chairman of their department. Stephen Franklyn.'

'With a "y",' Mac added. 'Do you think he has anything to do with this?'

'I don't know, but it all does seem to tie back to Riverside. Boy, is Hutchinson going to be pissed about this. This is not going to help with the fund-raising.'

TEN

Given the time difference and the fact that they had to change planes on the way back, it was mid-afternoon by the time they landed at LaGuardia and late afternoon by the time they returned to Mac's apartment.

Mackenzie was exhausted, and seriously wondered how she was going to get through the classes and meetings she had scheduled for tomorrow, and then to the sale at Bartholomew's. But if she did, maybe she could sleep in on Saturday. The prospect sounded blissful.

Chad spent virtually all of Friday at Mackenzie's apartment, making the first round of the many phone calls to the people and labs Vandeveere and the FBI had referred him to. He wasn't exactly eager, but he was curious to see just how much it was going to cost him to test his new-found collection. He had an initial conclusion by Friday afternoon. It was going to cost a lot.

By the time she and Chad were leaving for the Bartholomew's sale just before five on Friday afternoon, Mackenzie was extremely grateful for the restorative powers of cosmetics and caffeine.

She and Lieutenant Buratti had missed one another by phone a few times, but on the last round of messages, she'd managed to let him know that she and Chad would be at the Bartholomew's sale. If he needed to, he could reach her there.

Having decided that it was foolish even to try to hail a cab at five o'clock on a Friday afternoon, Mac and Chad headed for the Lexington Avenue line, and took the subway to 68th Street, and then walked the two blocks to the Bartholomew's building on 69th Street just off Park.

If they didn't already know it was a special occasion at Bartholomew's, the line of limousines waiting to discharge their passengers would have been a good tip-off. The impression of this being a major event carried through to the interior, where the glittering crowd mingled in the large lobby near a special draped bar area before heading off to inspect the sale in the large T-shaped exhibition space.

Chad leaned down and said softly into her ear, 'I think you can safely say this is an A-list crowd. I just saw two people I recognized from seeing their picture in the *Times* Arts and Leisure section last week.'

Mac looked at him and nodded her agreement. She had been to some dazzling gatherings, of course, but not as many in the last few years, and not too many in New York. She was feeling somewhat underdressed, despite the fact that she was wearing one of those outfits that the fashion magazines say can go effortlessly from work to cocktails to the poshest event with just a change of accessories. The fashion magazines lie.

Chad decided to brave the crowd near the bar, and left

Mac to stand by herself for a while. As she looked around, Mackenzie thought about her sudden immersion in the world of art. This art community was, in fact, a different world. The term 'world' is used frequently – the automotive world, the academic world, the entertainment world, as though to denote a separate sphere. But the term 'art world' is unusually apropos, for these people, Mac was learning, truly lived in a different orbit. As a child of privilege, she was accustomed to being around people who had never given a moment's thought to their economic security. It had always been a given. But this gathering was unlike anything else she'd ever seen, even among her parents' wealthiest friends. In a town where there were still homeless on the streets, where many professional people had accepted continuing economic anxiety as a fact of life, when the news was spouting about the average household's buying power being down, there were people here who would be spending thousands of dollars on a whim, tens of thousands on a hunch, and hundreds of thousands, if not millions, on the evening's prizes. It was indeed another world.

Chad returned with a white-wine spritzer and a man in tow, a gentleman about her age, she guessed, with a prematurely receding hairline. 'Mackenzie, say hello to Arthur Healy. He's the friend Tom Vandeveere told us about.'

Mackenzie offered her hand. 'Of course. How nice to meet you. Did Tom say you were with Bartholomew's, Arthur?'

'Good God, no. I'm here out of curiosity about the Bradford collection like everybody else. It's worthwhile

169

taking a look at it, if you haven't already, by the way. But I came over because Tom asked me to keep an eye out, and to congratulate Chad on joining the brotherhood.'

Mac raised her eyebrows quizzically.

'Arthur owns a gallery down in center-city Philadelphia,' Chad explained. 'And if you have some words of wisdom to pass on to me, Arthur, I'm ready to hear them, especially given the past week.'

'The best advice I know about art actually came out of Hollywood, believe it or not,' Healy said. 'And it's this: Nobody knows anything. There's no telling about taste in this world any more. It's like even the definition of what's good art is controlled by the PR types these days.' He moved slightly towards the wall so he could set down his wine glass and leave his hands free. It was obvious that Arthur talked with his hands. 'One guy I know – I don't handle his stuff – but he's this real blustery, good-looking, picture-in-*Vanity-Fair* type. What everybody thinks is the artist type. But I tell you, his work is like two steps away from paint by numbers. *Borinnng*. Predictable.' He reached for his glass before an efficient white-jacketed waiter swept it away, then set it down again when it was safe. 'This other guy. I don't handle him either, although I would give my right arm to, you know? His technique is so superb it absolutely disappears.' He looked off into the air, as if picturing the work he was talking about. 'Whatever he paints, it's like you're looking at it for the first time. Fresh. One of my old teachers said real art gives you a new way of looking at things, and that's what this guy does. But if you ran into him at a party, no, you wouldn't run into him at a party because he doesn't go. If you ran into him at the post office or the hardware store, you'd think he was maybe an accountant. So the PR types don't like him, so the buzz isn't there, so the big checkbooks don't open. It tears my heart out, I tell you, what heart I have left, that is.'

'Given recent events, I was already rethinking my decision to buy the gallery, Arthur,' Chad said. 'And now you've managed to trample the small hope I had left.'

Mac looked over towards the main door, and saw that Lieutenant Buratti was just coming in. She caught his eye with a wave, and he walked toward her. Chad excused himself from Healy and joined them.

'Hey, Chad, how you doin',' Buratti said in greeting. 'I can only stay a few minutes, but I wanted to fill you in. The FBI guy, Daly, was a help and he says if we can come up with anything on the deaths in Seattle or Tulsa that seem to tie in, he'll get involved. He seems to be taking this a little more seriously, unlike your Chief Karlman, who was unimpressed. He's now running special ballistics tests on the fragments they dug out of Howard. The guy is definitely a meatball, I tell ya. Anyway, I talked to the cops out in Seattle and in Tulsa, and I just heard back from Tulsa about an hour ago. In fact, it was the cop who wrote up the report that called me on that one. It's still classified as a hit and run, but he said there was something funny about it the whole time. From eyewitness reports, the van that ran this Noble kid down, it was like it was aiming for him. Picked up speed and took him out. The other thing he'd noted in the report was that the witnesses said the license plate was obscured with mud, even though the back of the van seemed to be clean.'

'How about Seattle?' Mac asked.

'When I first called up there, they weren't too thrilled about pulling the files out, but I called back after I talked to the Tulsa guy and that seems to have put a little fire under them. I'll check back on Monday.' Buratti's gaze drifted to the left, and then he did a double-take as he looked toward the *hors d'oeuvres* table longingly. 'Lord, keep me away from there.' He looked back to Chad, then patted his inside jacket pocket and pulled out a small notebook. 'As to Lord Boleigh, the word I get is the same. This guy is buying heavy in seventeenth- and early-eighteenth-century furniture and decorative arts. Does that mean anything to you?'

'Does it have any particular meaning?' Chad asked in reply. 'No. It just tells me what he's buying.'

'Me, I still have trouble figuring out which century is which. It's like I have to stop and say, "Okay, it's nineteen hundred something, and that's the twentieth century, so the eighteenth century must mean seventeen hundred something." Takes a lot of time, y'know?' He eyed the *hors d'oeuvres* table again. 'Maybe I'll just wander over and see if they have any carrot sticks.'

'Mario,' Mac said in a cautionary tone.

As Buratti stepped toward the food, both Mackenzie and Chad heard their names called out. Not recognizing the voice immediately, Mac turned to see President Hutchinson heading toward them, Stephen Franklyn trailing behind. Chad groaned loudly enough that she was concerned they might hear him, but then she realized the din of the crowd was sufficient to cover.

'How nice to see you at an event like this, Mackenzie,'

Hutchinson said to her. 'Am I to assume that now that your brother's in the art world, we'll be seeing more of you at such functions?'

'I'm not making any promises on that, sir. Hello, Stephen,' she said.

'Good evening,' Franklyn said, sounding remarkably if unintentionally like Alfred Hitchcock.

'To what do we owe the honor of your presence, Stephen,' Chad said, and Mackenzie almost choked on her spritzer.

'Stephen's here in his capacity as an advisor to the Riverside Collection,' Hutchinson explained. 'Mr Bradford was a good friend to Riverside for many years, though he wasn't an alumni. And we had hoped he might bequeath something directly to the school, but that's not to be. Although Riverside will be receiving a portion of tonight's proceeds, if only a small portion. But there is a painting in his collection that we've coveted for years. We decided some time ago to acquire it for the Riverside Collection if and when Bradford ever sold it.'

'And what's that, sir?' Chad asked.

Franklyn answered. 'A seventeenth-century painting of King John signing the Magna Carta. The work is quite fine, even though the painter didn't live long enough to establish much of a reputation. Troublesome times in England, you know. It was painted in 1638—'

'The year Riverside was founded,' interrupted Hutchinson.

' – and I think it was the Cromwellians who got him.'

Mackenzie saw Buratti heading back toward their group and edged to the side. She inspected the small plate of goodies he'd brought back with him. 'Very good, Lieutenant,' she said. 'I assume that's a low-cal dip for the veggies?'

'That's what they promised.' He held the plate up for her. 'Help yourself if you want some.'

She did pick up a beautiful piece of yellow pepper, which was every bit as sweet as she hoped it would be. She glanced over her shoulder to see that Chad was still trapped with Franklyn and Hutchinson. Hutchinson gave a courtly dip of his head to someone in the crowd he'd just recognized. The man was smooth, she had to admit.

'Now what the hell is he doing here?' she heard Buratti say. 'Tell me this guy's suddenly got culture.'

'Who?' Mac said, trying to follow Buratti's line of vision. She saw an older gentleman, perhaps in his late sixties, who had paused on the single stair that led into the room. He was quite dapper looking, wearing a lightweight gray chesterfield coat and the kind of hat that her great-uncle used to wear. A fedora? Maybe that's what it was called. Whatever it was, it looked terrific on this man. He wasn't very tall, maybe only an inch or two over her five-six, but his posture gave the impression of greater height, and his silvery gray hair, which he smoothed back after removing his hat, was quite a headful. A young man hovered near his right shoulder, obviously ready to assist the older man if he needed help with the step.

'Who is he?' Mac said again to Buratti.

'Gianni di Luca, also known as Johnny Lucky, also known as Mr Lucky. The only retired capo I know of, so maybe he is Mr Lucky.' Buratti caught the eye of a passing

waiter and handed him his now-empty plate. 'Not too many of them get to collect their social security, y'know. He's out of New England. Not Boston, but Providence maybe. He stepped down a few years ago, and I haven't heard much about him. So maybe he's taken up art in his retirement. Whaddya think?' He said the last in a tone that indicated he thought that was unlikely. 'Let me know if he gets involved in this, would you, Mac? I'm just curious.'

'You're heading out now?'

'Yeah. It's been a long week. Glad it's Friday night.' He patted his pockets down, since it had been his habit to light up a cigarette as soon as he got outdoors again. He looked her straight in the eye. 'I'm going to stop doing this one day, I swear. See you, Mac. Talk to you Monday if not before.'

She rejoined Chad and Stephen Franklyn. 'I was just telling Chadwick, Mackenzie, that Lord Boleigh will be joining us as well,' Franklyn said. 'He's the most significant contributor to the Riverside Collection, you know.'

'And that's not all you said,' Chad prompted.

It didn't take much to get Franklyn to repeat himself, after he checked around to make sure Hutchinson wasn't within earshot. 'I was telling your brother that I've heard Boleigh has gone absolutely bananas' – with his accent, that came out ba-NAH-nas – 'buying up seventeenth- and eighteenth-century furnishings. He's shipping them from all over the world back to the ancestral home, and I've heard that he thinks if he can surround himself with authentic materials of the time, allowing absolutely nothing modern within the house, that he'll be able to time travel.' Franklyn started to giggle. It was not an attractive sound.

'Just another example of somebody having a little too much time and a lot too much money on his hands, I say,' Chad said. 'Speak of the devil.'

Mac looked in the direction that Chad indicated and saw Hutchinson and Lord Boleigh joining the crowd that was starting toward the auditorium.

'Shall we?' Chad said, and the three joined the throng.

Mackenzie had never been to an auction before, not on this level. There had been one fund-raiser when she was in college, but the auctioneer in that case was a fellow student, and he had none of the sense of theater that tonight's auctioneer had on the stand.

And theater was what it was. The auditorium was set up like a theater, with rows of comfortable seating leading up the gently raked carpeted floor. The stage area, where the items to be auctioned were displayed on a revolving circular platform, was divided into three viewing compartments. The stage and the front of the auditorium, where the auctioneer stood to the right, also had the benefit of stage lighting, and somebody had gone to a great deal of effort to individualize lighting selections for each of the objects shown. As the stage revolved to bring the next object around for viewing, the lights would dim. When the lights were brought up again, they were subtly different, highlighting the current object as dramatically as possible.

Mac leaned over to Chad and asked if she were really seeing lighting changes for every piece. 'Computers,' Arthur Healy, who had joined them again for the auction, whispered back to her.

The collection was every bit as eclectic as Vandeveere had said it would be, possibly more so. In addition to the paintings and the furnishings, there was a small collection of Greek vases and a smaller collection of Roman bronzes. Broadening the range even more was the fact that it also included several pieces of Western art which had apparently adorned Mr Bradford's personal library, and a collection of porcelains that had apparently been collected by Mrs Bradford in the first half of the century, a collection that was rivaled only by the Fabergé eggs for delicacy and detail.

From where Mac was sitting, she could see Franklyn, Hutchinson and Lord Boleigh rather well, and she was astonished when Boleigh kept the bidding going on a tall dresser, which the catalogue dated *circa* 1725. It was presumed to have been made in England, and the Bradford files traced its history back to its importation to Boston in 1730. It was, as the auctioneer dramatically stated, an important piece.

Apparently. Lord Boleigh ended up paying seven hundred and fifty thousand dollars for it, which, Chad told her, would mean eight hundred twenty five thousand with commission. A nice little addition for the bedroom.

The bidding was quite energetic all evening. Some items disappeared in sales so quick that Mac didn't have time to look them up in the catalogue. The Riverside Collection did get the painting Hutchinson wanted, with Stephen Franklyn handling the bidding paddle. Franklyn looked bored while the bidding was going on, and he sounded bored when Chad congratulated him later.

There wasn't a pattern evident among any of the buyers

present, at least none that Arthur Healy could determine. Winning bids seemed to be spread throughout the audience. A number of items went to a bidder on the phone, but it was impossible to tell if it was the same bidder consistently. As to identifying a collector who was buying pieces that reflected the collection Chad had happened upon, that proved to be impossible.

The auctioneer used his theatrical sense well throughout the sale, and kept up the energy and the interest in the room throughout the evening. It paid off handsomely, for the sale exceeded all estimates. At the end, its total came to over twenty-two million dollars, which included the quarter of a million Riverside paid for the painting of King John and the Magna Carta.

Mackenzie found both figures astonishing, and told Chad as much when they were getting into a cab on Park Avenue. 'A quarter of a million dollars for a painting for the Riverside collection. Come on, wasn't it two weeks ago he was busting chops all night to raise that much for the scholarship account?'

'Different funds,' Chad said by way of explanation as he stifled a yawn.

'Still, I think twenty-two million for a collection no one's heard of is pretty amazing.'

'I think you're right, there. Even the pre-sale estimate put the total at only about fifteen million,'

'Listen to us. *Only* fifteen million,' Mac said, then drifted off into looking at the Christmas decorations that already twinkled in some store windows.

By the time the cab pulled up to her apartment, they were

making plans about just how late they could sleep in. Chad was planning on heading back to Registon tomorrow, but, as he said, there wasn't any law that said he had to take the early train.

The light on the answering machine was blinking when they got into the apartment, and Mac hoped she hadn't missed another call from Peter.

She had. 'Mac, what the hell is going on?' His voice came into the room, and this time it was evident he was on international lines. 'Rachel told me you were going out to New Mexico but you'd be back by now. She said you were working on some kind of investigation with Chad.' Rachel had an unfortunate talent for the dramatic. Mac should have remembered that before she gave her any information whatsoever. 'You aren't into anything dangerous are you, Mackenzie? Mackenzie?' The repetition was for effect, she could tell. 'I'll try you late Sunday night your time or early Monday morning. I miss you.' The machine beeped that the message was over and she was about to reset it when it beeped again.

'Mackenzie, Tom Vandeveere here.' Mac paused the machine and called for Chad to join her to listen. He walked in, pulling off his tie. 'I thought Chad might still be in New York and I wanted to get this information to you as quickly as possible. I was finally able to speak to Angelo Campanelli this afternoon, and he's agreed to see you tomorrow morning.' They looked at each other, both faces turned into masks of disappointment. There went the plans for sleeping in. Mac shoved a small pad toward her brother when Vandeveere started to give detailed directions to

179

Campanelli's place in northern New Jersey. 'I'm still checking on a few other things, and hope to have that information for you as soon as possible. I'll hope to speak with you then. Oh, by the way, Beth is fine,' he added as an afterthought before hanging up.

Mac switched off the machine and moved the phone toward her brother. 'Here. Good luck trying to find us a rental car for tomorrow. I'm going to bed.'

ELEVEN

Chad was able to locate one of the few rental cars left in Manhattan on an autumn Saturday. But Mac had to laugh when he drove around the corner to pick her up. It was a boat of a luxury car, far bigger than anything Chad was used to driving. His discomfort showed as he tried to pull up to the kerb and left a full yard between it and the tires. And when he tried to unlock the passenger side door it was the window that opened instead.

It made for a comfortable ride, however. And while the day wasn't clear, it was at least dry, and the last bits of fall color were visible along the sides of the road. The temperature was in the mid-thirties when they left the city.

Campanelli lived in the middle of New Jersey's horse country, where the beautiful rolling countryside was dotted with stately colonial homes. The directions Vandeveere had given were precise and accurate. As they made the final turn up Campanelli's long curving driveway, Mac remarked, 'I'm not sure I understood from Tom what this Campanelli guy does. But whatever he does, he does well at it.'

The home was a gracious two-story colonial, and the long

circular driveway, which curved in front of the house and then led again back out to the road with a detour to the garage area and the side of the house, was fenced with plain white wooden boards.

Chad parked the car to the side of the driveway, where he hoped it would be out of the way. It took a few tries to get it far enough to the side, however, and finally Mackenzie had to get out of the car to give him the final guidance. He hoped this Campanelli guy wasn't watching out the window. It was embarrassing enough without witnesses.

The door was almost covered with a beautiful harvest wreath, and the doorbell they rang sounded with a reverberating chime inside. After a few moments, Angelo Campanelli himself opened the door.

Angelo Campanelli had been baptized Michelangelo, and his mother called him that until the day she died. When he decided to make his living in the world of art, however, he found the full name more of a burden than an advantage.

Young Michelangelo was all for advantages. He'd grown up, after all, believing all those things his mother had whispered in his ear from the time he was a baby. But, as important as his mother had been in his upbringing, he really took after his father in one important aspect – little Michelangelo, too, believed the world was made for him. The mature Angelo had developed enough awareness, however, and had enough personal charm, that he was able to contain his exuberant self-confidence from bloating into arrogance. But it was something he had to be alert to every day.

Now in his late forties, he'd finally come into his own in the last ten years, receiving the respect he deserved. Angelo fancied himself quite a dresser, quite a dancer, quite a lover, and quite the man of art. And now, with a professional of Tom Vandeveere's reputation actually referring people to him, well, no doubt it was going to be a good day. He adjusted the silk cravat he wore and opened the door.

The house inside was every bit as tasteful as the outside and the grounds, Mac thought to herself. Then she realized again that of course it would be. This was the home of yet another art professional.

They entered into a wide central hall. The area was dominated by a large but simple chandelier. A beautiful side table sat to the right, with a large oval mirror on the wall above it. The mirror reflected the fire in the room to the left, which is where Campanelli guided them.

'It was a little chilly this morning, so I thought a fire might help.' He gestured to a large silver tray set with a coffee service. 'May I offer you some coffee?'

Both Chad and Mac accepted, and they took seats on one of the two loveseats that sat on either side of the fireplace.

'Tom Vandeveere told me you were going to the Bradford sale last night,' Campanelli said as he gave Mac her coffee cup. He looked at Chad. 'You said cream only, no sugar, right?'

'Yes to both,' Chad answered.

'One of my pieces was in that sale,' Campanelli offered as he came back with Chad's cup.

'One of your pieces?' Mac asked. 'How do you mean?'

'One of the pieces I . . . brokered' – Campanelli had obviously chosen the word carefully – 'was part of the Bradford collection.'

'I thought this collection was some thirty or forty years old,' Mac said, 'and you certainly haven't been in the business since you were a toddler.'

Campanelli acknowledged her compliment with a nod. 'Most of Mr Bradford's collection was acquired some years ago, that's true, and he hasn't been an active buyer for some time. But the piece I was able to come up with was quite special.'

'Which was it, if you don't mind my asking,' said Chad.

'Sorry,' Campanelli said. 'It would be a breach of confidence. Most of my work is confidential.'

Chad sipped his coffee, puzzled. He was still trying to figure out what that work was. Mac was trying to figure out why this guy's unctuous charm made her so nervous.

'So what is it that I can help you with, Mr Griffin? Vandeveere didn't explain too much in our conversation.'

Chad started to unzip the soft-sided briefcase he'd brought with him, which contained the bags of photos. 'A few weeks ago I bought the River's End Gallery over in Registon from Malcolm Howard,' he started.

'Malcolm Howard, my God, I just heard about him last week! I'd been out of town since the end of October. And you'd just bought the gallery from him? Extraordinary!'

Mac's bullshit detector started to sound in her brain. She knew instinctively the guy was lying, but she wasn't sure about what.

'A few days after Mr Howard died, I discovered some additional inventory,' Chad continued, being careful not to look at Mackenzie, hoping she wouldn't comment on his inventive turn of phrase. 'Unfortunately, there aren't any records on these items, and Tom Vandeveere suggested that you might be able to help us identify some of them. Apparently you did some business with Malcolm Howard?'

'Yes, Malcolm was a client. A very good client. Had been for a number of years. I was able to help him out when his customers wanted to . . . acquire certain items.' Again, Mac noticed the hesitation. 'Although we didn't do that much in the last year or so. I think he was devoting more of his time to one client, one who wasn't in need of my services.'

'What exactly is it that you do, Mr Campanelli?' Mackenzie asked. Chad tensed up next to her. He was dying to know the same thing, but wasn't sure she should have asked the question – yet.

He smiled, reached for his coffee, took a leisurely sip, replaced the cup, and looked her directly in the eye. 'I like to think of myself as an impresario of the art world. I bring together talented individuals and people who are interested in using their talents.'

'Using their talents how?'

'Some of my clients commission certain works, for example.'

'Certain original works, or copies of other works?' Mac saw the alarm in Chad's eyes as she asked the question, but she realized the only way to get an answer out of this guy was to push, and push hard.

'Copies?' he said, trying to appear shocked. 'How do you mean, copies?'

'Copies like in forgeries.'

'Trade in forgeries? Absolutely not. That would be wrong.' He sat back and adjusted his jacket behind him. 'I have been able to assist some museums in obtaining security copies of their paintings, however. But that I hardly call forgery.'

'You mean some of the paintings that are on exhibition in museums around here are copies that you arranged for?' Chad asked.

'Museums here and across the country. And Paris. And London.' Campanelli's pride got the better of him and he couldn't resist showing off.

Chad pulled the photographs out and explained the three groupings to Campanelli. The impresario moved forward on the loveseat until his knees were almost touching the table that sat between them. He started going through the pictures slowly.

'I assume Tom told you of the problems of looking at photographs,' he said to Chad.

'Yes, I know there's no way you can tell much about the pieces. What I'm trying to find out is if you recognize any of them, if you can give me anything to go on.'

Mac was watching Campanelli intently, and she saw his eyes widen when he looked closely at one picture in particular in the first group of photos. She couldn't tell what it was precisely that he was looking at, only that it was in the collection of the Greek and Roman material. He said nothing. He looked through the second grouping, the photos of the six paintings, and he set aside the picture of the fake Monet. When he looked through the third group, the one that contained such a mixture of items, Mac watched as his eyes flared in recognition at least twice. Again he said nothing.

He piled the pictures carefully, and handed them back to Chad, except for the one he had set aside. 'This,' he said. 'This I recognize. If I'm not mistaken, the canvas is much smaller than the work it copies, no?'

Chad nodded yes.

'It was a stupid idea, and I tried to tell Malcolm at the time, but he had this customer who wanted a damn lilyscape, and she wanted it to fit a particular wall. I protested, but she made a generous offer. I knew it wouldn't work, because part of the grace of those paintings is their size. I'm not surprised to see it sitting in Malcolm's back room.'

Chad started returning the photos to the briefcase, slipping the picture of the phony Monet in the proper place. 'One last thing, and then we'll get out of your way. Do you know anything about a belt—'

'A fan belt, I think it is,' Mac interrupted quickly. 'It was making a terrible noise after we got off the highway.' She looked at Chad with a blink of her eye, trying to tell him to wipe the amazed expression off his face. 'Could you tell us where the nearest service station might be, so we could have it fixed before we get back on the road?'

Chad tried to pick up the cue. 'Yeah, it would help if we had somebody take a look at it.' Jeez, he hoped that didn't sound as lame to Campanelli's ears as it did to his.

Campanelli offered to draw them a map to guide them to the service station and back to the highway, and he got up to

187

fetch some paper from his desk at the far end of the room. Chad and Mac indulged in a conversation of raised eyebrows and furtive glances, the end result of which was 'We'll talk later.'

Later turned out to be after they'd driven down Campanelli's long driveway and made the first turn off his road. 'So what the hell was that all about?' Chad said. 'The fan belt?'

'He was lying,' Mac said. 'I know he was lying. He recognized at least two more of those pieces and he said nothing about them. And the Monet? What did he really tell you that you didn't know? You knew that was a fake the minute you looked at it.' She looked over at him apologetically. 'And the fan belt was the best I could come up with.'

'Actually, I thought it was pretty ingenious, once I caught on to what you were doing. And once I stopped tripping over my own tongue. So what's next?'

'Does it strike you that we've talked to a lot of people, and we've gotten a lot more information, but we still don't have a clue who it is we're looking for?'

Chad drummed his fingers on the steering wheel. 'Yeah, that about sums it up. So what do we do now?'

'Buratti tells me that when he gets stuck he goes back to the beginning. So maybe we should go back to the gallery. Or to New London.'

'Now?' Chad asked.

'You put your bag in the car, right? And you were going to take the train up later today anyway. Let's drive up and I can bring the car back to the city whenever.' Mac glanced around. 'If I can get used to driving something this big.'

Chad looked at his watch. 'Hey, you know, if I don't watch the speed limit exactly, we could maybe make it in time for a late lunch.'

TWELVE

They pulled in to their parents' driveway at 1:15, 'just before the kitchen closed' according to Stella. She greeted them at the kitchen door with big hugs for both of them, which was unusually demonstrative for Stella. The last ten days of those 'skulking strangers' must be getting to her, Mac thought.

Their parents were welcoming as well, and sat at the table with them while Stella plied them with sandwiches and one of her autumn specialties, apple brown betty. Tasting the dessert, Mac rolled her eyes and told Stella it was worth the drive.

Chad saw the security guard in the driveway and went out to let the guard know he was back. They could go to the nights-only schedule now.

Their parents excused themselves back to their studies, and Chad picked up the coffee pot on his way back to the table, pouring for his sister and himself. Then he tried to coax Mac into a discussion of the afternoon's schedule. 'You said we should start back at the beginning. Does that mean we have to physically go back to the storage space?'

'No, I don't think so. Why don't we do this? Let's go sit

at the dining-room table so we'll be out of Stella's way, and we'll write down everything we know about all that stuff in New London. Everything we've learned from Buratti, from Tom Vandeveere, from Jarvi, from whoever. And we'll just look at it.'

'Ah, the time of synthesis.'

'The what?' Mac said, starting to pick up their dishes. Stella was off for her afternoon nap and it would never do to leave her kitchen messy.

'Trying to pull things together into a cohesive whole,' Chad explained. 'What one of my grad-school teachers called the time of synthesis.'

'That's as good a term as any. No offense, but I'd just like to get this time over so I can go back to my own life without goons showing up to conk me on the head or go through my underwear. Not that it hasn't been a thrill spending so much time with you, little brother.'

Chad got up and headed to the key rack near the back door, then remembered he had the keys to the rental car in his pocket. 'Why don't you get us set up, and I'm going to run down to the post office and pick up my mail before they close. Okay?'

Mac had just finished tidying the kitchen and was about to call her apartment to check her messages when she heard a car pull up the driveway, much faster than usual. She peeked out the window to see that it was Chad. He'd left the car running and was hurrying to the door.

'What's up?' she said, holding the door open a bit.

Chad pulled the storm door open and walked past her. 'Something weird's going on – for a change. I just ran into

Sarah Davis, the decorator, at the post office. And she reams into me for hiring another decorator.' He walked to the opposite end of the table and started going through the pile of his things he'd left there. 'If I wanted to use someone else, she says, I could have had the courtesy to just tell her and not make up some exotic story.' He hadn't found what he was looking for yet, and he impatiently shoved the pile to the side. 'So I asked her what the hell she was talking about, and she says she saw the van from Decorators of New England sitting outside the gallery most of the day. Only she couldn't remember if it was most of the day yesterday or Thursday.' He finally found what he was looking for, and held up a set of keys. 'I was going to stop on my way back, but I left the keys here.' He started for the door. 'Want to come with me?'

'Sure,' Mac said. 'Why not?'

All looked well as they pulled up to the kerb and walked to the gallery. It wasn't until they were actually inside that you could tell something was seriously wrong. Chad led the way through the front gallery, which seemed fine. The middle gallery is where the problem started. 'Oh, shit,' he said from the archway that connected the two rooms, 'would you look at this.' He strode across the room to its rear wall.

Mac had just made it into the middle gallery by that time. As Chad bent down to see where the paneling, including the skirting boards, had been pried way from the wall, he caught a glimpse of the small hallway that led to the office. It was virtually destroyed.

He sat back on his haunches and slipped to the floor. 'Oh, *shiit*,' he said emphatically. 'Mac, look at this.'

She did. The hallway was only about eight feet long, the office door was on the near left side and further back to the right was the door to the bathroom. Opposite that was the door to the small storeroom. The top half of the walls here, like in the gallery areas were, or had been, plaster. This part of the building hadn't been touched in years, so plasterboard was not in evidence. The lower half of the walls was beautiful maple paneling, with a horizontal strip of maple at just about chair height. That horizontal strip of wood was all that was left of the walls now. The plaster had been knocked out, and the paneling pried away. The old frame of the walls was visible like a skeleton. Rubble was piled in the hallway, but had been swept to one side with a broom that was still propped against the wall.

'Do you *believe* this,' Chad said to Mac, shaking his head.

She tried her best to cheer him up. 'The good news is that they seem to have found what they were looking for as soon as they got into the middle gallery. Imagine if the whole place looked like this.'

Chad pushed himself to his feet. 'I thought Karlman was keeping an eye on this place. This isn't some five minutes in and out here, somebody put a lot of time into this. I'm gonna call him right now.'

Chad picked his way across the rubble that sat in front of the office door and made his way to the phone. It took about ten minutes for Karlman to show up. Mac had to remind Chad a few times not to touch anything, in order to allow Karlman the full effect of what had happened.

Karlman, it turned out, was not surprised. 'Yeah, my guys told me about the decorator. Was it Thursday or yesterday they was here? I can check for you,' he said accommodatingly. 'I thought it was a little strange, but I know you're under pressure to get open, too.'

'The bad news is that I didn't hire a decorator, Chief. And you can see what they did.'

Karlman peeked around the corner to the middle gallery. 'They weren't supposed to do that?'

Chad shook his head no.

'Son of a bitch! The officer checked their work order and everything. Let me call him on this. I'll see what I can find out and let you know. Are you going to be here a while?'

Mac answered. 'No, we'll be over at the home number. You can reach us there.'

It took a little cajoling, but Mac got Chad out of there within a few minutes. He pounded the steering wheel a few times on the short drive home, kicked some gravel in the driveway as they walked to the kitchen door, and he started pacing the kitchen once they got inside. Mac watched while he vented his anger as best he could.

'You understand what I mean, Mac?' he said to her mid-pace. 'These people – whoever they are – they've taken over my life for the last two weeks, and I'm sick of it, I'm just sick of it. It's got to stop. They've come after me, they've come after you, they followed us to New Mexico . . .'

Mac briefly turned psychologist. 'Okay, Chad, I agree with you, with everything you've said. But getting mad isn't going to do the job. We still have to figure out who is doing this.'

'And how do you propose to do that?' he said with a bit of a challenge.

'Like I talked about before, we're going to sit down and go over everything we know, everything we've learned in the last two weeks. Maybe we'll see some kind of a pattern, maybe we've missed something. Maybe sitting down and *calmly* looking at everything will get us started on the right path.

'Okay,' Mac said as she picked up the pens and the four by six cards she'd borrowed from her father's office and moved into the dining room and its larger table. She wasn't the child of academics for nothing. She knew how to organize research. She dealt out over half the pack of cards to Chad. 'You start on the information about the material in the storage locker. Everything we know.'

The phone rang two times, and shortly their father appeared in the doorway of the dining room. 'Chadwick. It's a Mr Thomason Vandeveere for you.'

Chad looked at Mac with a raise of the eyebrow. 'I'll take it in the other room. Why don't you get on the kitchen phone?' he said.

'Chad?' Tom Vandeveere said. 'How did it go this morning?'

'That's a long story,' Chad said. 'And Mac thinks he knows more than he's telling us.'

'With Campanelli, that's a distinct possibility,' Vandeveere said. 'I'm calling for a reason, and I'm sorry this took longer than I thought. I knew exactly where to find what I was looking for in my reference books in New York, but unfortunately I couldn't find the exact books here. At any rate, the picture I kept, my initial impression was right. Remember my telling you about all those World War II souvenirs showing up? I think that's the case here. From the pictures I've found, I'm pretty sure this is a fragment from one of the cathedrals that was damaged in the bombings in East Germany. Given the pictures that I've looked at, I'm not sure which cathedral. There are a couple it could have come from. But I'm almost positive that's what it is. This kind of figure usually represents the damned writhing in the fires of hell.'

'See?' Mac said. 'I wasn't far off. It was meant to scare people.'

Vandeveere laughed across the miles.

'Thanks, Tom,' Chad said. 'That's a big help because we're just setting down to summarize everything we've found out.'

'And, just to let you know, I've tried to call the two dealers who specialize in the Greek and Roman, but I won't be able to reach them until next week apparently. I'll let you know when I do. But give me a call if I can be of any more help,' Vandeveere said.

'Tom?' Mac said quickly before he could get off the phone. 'How's Beth doing?'

He hesitated on the answer. 'She's fine. She's doing just fine.'

'Is it me,' Mac said as they walked back into the dining room, 'or did it sound to you like they're getting under one another's skin, as in irritation.'

'I don't know,' said Chad. 'Maybe if we figure out what's going on, we can spring Beth and she can go back home.'

'Okay,' Mac said, taking her seat. 'You've got another piece of information for your collection. Now let's start to write.'

197

Mackenzie summarized what they learned on headlined index cards – mainly what Buratti had gleaned for them, she realized.

Chad bitched and moaned a bit, complaining that he had much more to do than she did. He finally decided, after a few false starts, to group the pieces together where possible and not even try to deal with some of the individual pieces.

They worked in relative silence for over a half-hour. When Mac sat back and put her pen down, she saw that they had cards spread all over the table.

Mac got up to fix coffee while Chad finished. She walked back into the room to see Chad staring at the cards. The afternoon sun was shining in, from the river side of the room, and its soft golden light filled the dining room.

'Okay,' she said, leaving the swinging door open so she'd be able to hear when the coffee stopped dripping. 'What do we know? We know that Malcolm Howard was killed two weeks ago today, by a shot to the back of his head. We know that in the twenty-four hours before his death he was busy trying to convey to you certain pieces of information, trying to give you access to his safe deposit box and storage area, and leaving you a cryptic note that says "he must be stopped".'

'He couldn't have put in another syllable, right? Or initials?' Chad's frustration was taking its toll.

'We also know that in the day or two prior to that, a young man was killed in Tulsa who had apparently been doing business with Howard, and this killing of people might be what he – Howard – was referring to stopping. Because we also know that another young man who was doing business with Howard may or may not have been killed earlier. But we still don't know who the "he" refers to. Conclusion: none so far.'

'Is this supposed to be encouraging?' Chad said glumly.

'We know that a couple of goons roughed you up, inquiring after a certain object apparently belonging to someone referred to as His Lordship. Said goons apparently are the same ones who came after me a few days later, identifying said object as a belt, and no one we know or have talked to has a clue as to what they might be talking about. Some people, in all likelihood the same goon-types, followed us to New Mexico, presumably under the impression that we would have said belt in our possession, and ransacked our hotel rooms looking for it. Conclusion: these goons are not operating on their own, but in fact are in someone's employ, because they have the money to get to New Mexico on short notice, which, as you know, since you're paying for my air fare, too, costs a few bucks. Corollary conclusion, having nothing to do with anything: one of them has busted olfactory connections because he wears enough cologne to make a horse weep.'

Chad rested his elbows on the table and his head in his hands. He was not the picture of energy.

Mac started walking back and forth to the kitchen through the still-open swinging door, bringing two mugs and some napkins on the first trip, a pitcher of milk and a trivet on the second, and the coffee pot on the third.

'We know that the jerks who attacked us referred to His Lordship wanting what's his, but the only Lordship we know is apparently buying heavily and exclusively in late

199

seventeenth- and eighteenth-century decorative arts, none of which fall into this particular puzzle. Anybody else you can think of that might be considered a Lordship?'

'Would somebody mistake Stephen Franklyn with his obnoxious accent for being low-level royalty?'

'Does Stephen Franklyn have the money to pull this off?' said Mac, answering a question with a question.

'I don't think so,' Chad replied. 'Have you seen the way he dresses?'

Mac nodded, silently agreeing with him. She pulled his mug toward her and poured the coffee. 'We know that Howard had a gambling problem, but the gamblers are sorry to see him dead, so they apparently didn't do it, but we don't know how he paid for his mother's upkeep in the pricey Riverside Park. We think that that weasel Campanelli may know more than he's telling, but who knows what that is. Have I missed anything?'

Chad shook his head. 'Not that I can think of.'

'You go next. How about summarizing the art situation.'

Mac looked up to see that her father had joined them. He was leaning against the side of the double-doored entrance to the dining room. 'Hi, Dad. Want some coffee?'

He declined her offer with a slight wave of his hand.

'We have,' Chad arranged the pictures in front of him, 'one item that we know is a fake, the quote unquote Monet painting. Five other paintings may or may not be forgeries, but my money is leaning on the side that says they are. The money that I'm going to have to spend having them examined and tested, that is.

'Next, we have a good-sized collection of Greek and

Roman objects, none of which are immediately discernible as fakes, most of which may be authentic. They range from vases and pitchers' – he adjusted the pictures in front of him – 'to statues of the gods, to a *really* good marble head of Dionysus, and various other things. According to Tom Vandeveere, this whole collection may have been a sideline that Howard was developing – legitimate or illegitimate, who knows – that didn't pan out.

'Next we have the mystery pile. We have a painting that looks like it's from the Venetian school, fifteenth century or thereabouts, which may or may not be authentic. We have a fifteenth-century map of the world, missing only a few details, like North and South America. We have a manuscript of the Gospels dated 1402, also known as the early fifteenth century. We have what looks like a small loom or model of a loom, year unknown. We have a metal thing, presumably Roman, function unidentified, that has fifteen something on it, and the word Augustus. And we now know, thanks to Tom Vandeveere, that the scarecrow, as you so colorfully called it, is one of the figures that adorned an East German cathedral until it was bombed off, presumably in 1945.'

Chad sat back in his chair. 'Like Vandeveere said when we were out there, except for the painting, it's hard to imagine that any of this mystery pile is fake. Who fakes an illuminated manuscript these days? Or am I just hanging out with the wrong crowd?'

'Do you have any ideas, Dad?' Mac said when she saw her father still standing in the doorway, puffing on his pipe.

'Have you had your mother look at the Roman piece yet?'

'No,' Chad said. 'I should have asked her that when I was writing this up.'

'Elizabeth,' Walker Griffin called. 'Come here, would you, dear? The children need your help.'

Elizabeth Griffin entered the dining room, removing her reading glasses as she did. 'What is it?'

'Mother, take a look at this photo, would you? Actually I have two,' he said, digging back into the bags. 'This one shows the inscription more clearly.'

'Chadwick, wherever did you get this?'

'Why,' he said, moving to stand behind her and peer over her shoulder. 'Do you know what it is?'

'Yes, it's a weight.'

'A weight? What's it for?'

'For trade. For balancing the scales, you know. Depending on what this weight is, if you went to the market to buy a half-pound of grapes, they'd put this on one side of the scales and the grapes on the other. It was a way for officials to keep their names before the public or for merchants to curry favor with the officials. Somewhat like those buttons or bumper stickers that people have today.'

'Can you tell what this one says?' Mac asked.

'Yes. This one looks like it was issued on the anniversary of the emperor Hadrian. They were frequently authorized as celebratory items, you see.'

'Why does it say augustus then?'

'Augustus was a title, bestowed by the senate, first on Octavius, better known as Augustus Caesar. Augustus means "the majestic". In this case, the weight was probably made by someone trying to flatter the emperor, cozy up. Hadrian never had the title augustus officially conferred.'

Mackenzie noticed that her father had stepped closer to the table, and he was re-arranging some of the cards she and Chad had written up and some of the photographs as well. 'What are you thinking, Dad?'

'Curious, it's just curious that's all,' he replied, pulling the pipe from his mouth. 'It's almost like you could take some of these and have an illustration for President Hutchinson's usual speech.'

Mackenzie felt the hairs on her arms stand up. She knew instinctively that he was absolutely right.

Chad was surprised at the comment. 'You mean the mission speech, the long one?'

Mackenzie got up and walked around the table to stand next to her father.

Walker Griffin had assembled the items in front of him. 'Look at this,' he said and moved a few of the photographs of the Greek items into place first. ' "From Plato's Academy of ancient Greece, where we witness the creation of that sacred relationship of teacher and student – " '

' " – a relationship that is still the guiding force of Riverside." ' Mackenzie echoed along with him.

He turned and gently lifted the picture of the weight his wife was still holding and placed it on the table. ' " – to the glories of the Roman empire, and its unquestionable heritage of civic pride, an empire which stretched across the known world, a world in which the proudest statement one could make was" ' – he looked at Mackenzie and Chad, and they joined him in the next phrase. ' "*Civus Romanus sum*. I am a Roman citizen." '

He pulled a photograph of the illuminated manuscript t
the center next. ' "The ludicrously misnamed Dark Ages
when the devoted scholarship of monks across Europe in fac
kept the flame of the ancient learnings alive, and preserve
for us all the teachings of Christianity, which was slowl
spreading across Europe from the Bosporus to the Britis
Isles, a faith which blossomed across the continent in th
form of magnificent cathedrals which dotted the land." ' Th
picture of the face of the damned took its place in line.

He paused, frowning, 'What's the line that starts th
Renaissance section?' he said to his wife.

' "We celebrate the Renaissance itself," ' she started, an
he picked up the phrasing immediately, ' "that inspired re
awakening and re-birth, that took man out of himself an
coaxed him to take a clear look at the universe and hi
place in it. Such immense talents of the Renaissance a
Brunelleschi and his principles of perspective" ' – the phot
of the Venetian painting was moved into place – ' "an
Galileo with his Scientific Treatises lit the flame of curiosit
that led to the world-expanding Age of Exploration." ' Th
photograph of the map of the world followed next. ' "Th
Age of Exploration became, of course, the Age of Discovery
which has a very personal meaning for those of us fortunat
enough to be part of the glorious American experiment."

'Let's see,' Walker Griffin said, 'the Age of Enlighten
ment is next, but I don't see anything that quite covers that
This little loom, of course, could stand in for the Industria
Revolution. And I'm afraid you fall short on the revolutio
in technology and communications as well. So maybe I'
mistaken.'

Mac and Chad stared at the pictures as their father had arranged them, then at each other.

Their mother interrupted the quiet. 'Excuse me, dears, but do you need me for anything else? I'm in the midst of some term papers.'

'No, Mother, thanks,' Chad said as she left the room. He went back to studying the arrangement of pictures his father had made. 'President Hutchinson in back of this whole thing?' He looked at Mac. 'Naaah,' he said, looking at his father and then back at his sister.

Mackenzie looked back down at the pictures, then at her father, and back at Chad again. 'You know, I think he might have something.'

'Come *on*, Mackenzie.'

'Remember what I was talking about on the plane out to New Mexico, that material on collectors I was reading? The collection is like a profile of a collector. Well, this collection could be a profile of Dr Hutchinson. We've been trying to figure out all week who might be behind all this. I think Dad just pointed it out.'

'Mackenzie, you can't be serious. There is no way I'm going to go up to Avery Hutchinson and accuse him of being behind assault, theft, *murder*, for God's sake! He's the president of the university!'

'I'm not saying we go and accuse him,' said Mac, moving back to her side of the table. 'I'm saying we don't dismiss it as a possibility. Look at what we have here. First, Hutchinson knew Malcolm Howard and knew him well, so he had access. Second, elements of this collection dovetail with what we know to be the driving force, the passion of

Hutchinson's life – the glories of Western civilization. In a way, that becomes some kind of motive. Third, Hutchinson has the money to support this kind of acquisition.'

'That's true,' Chad conceded. 'He's got more money than God.'

'And, in this case, money creates the opportunity.'

'What do you think, Dad?' Chad asked.

'I agree with both of you. Mackenzie's assessment of the overall situation is sound, but I tend to think you can't go up and accuse President Hutchinson without some concrete proof.'

'How do you think we could go about getting that?' Chad asked.

'Maybe if we get inside his house, and see what he's got in there?' Mac offered.

'*Break into his house?*' Chad asked, his voice practically squeaking. 'Oh, this is getting bizarre.'

'Hopefully not break in. Get in,' Mac clarified. 'If he is the collector behind this, I'm almost positive whatever collection he has would be in his house, because that's the kick for these people. To be able to have it close at hand, to look at it, to touch it, to know it's theirs. If we get in and find the collection we think we'll find, *then* we accuse him.'

'How do you propose we get in? Say "excuse me President Hutchinson, could we take a look around?" '

'Well, he isn't there this afternoon, I know that,' their father volunteered.

'He was at the auction last night,' Mac said. 'How do you know he's not back yet, Dad?'

206

'We were due to have a finance-committee meeting for the church this afternoon, before Reverend Whitcomb makes his report to the congregation tomorrow on having the bell tower redone. We were supposed to meet at Hutchinson's house, since he's the chairman. But he called around yesterday that we'd have to meet early Sunday morning, since he isn't due back until late tonight.'

'So we could go over now and knock on the door and the butler – what's his name?' Chad looked at Mac, but his father filled in the blank.

'Phillip.'

'Phillip would let us in?' he finished.

'Probably not,' Mac said.

'Not to aid you children in illegally or inappropriately entering someone's property, but this does seem to have a certain importance to it. What if I were to go over, ring the bell and engage Phillip in a brief conversation? Do you think that would be of help to your getting in, perhaps in the back?'

'Oh, Dad, that's a good idea,' Mac said. She looked at her father with new eyes. 'This is a whole new side of you we haven't seen before.'

Walker Griffin smiled at his daughter. 'Well, let me know when you want to go,' he said and he walked into the kitchen, pipe in hand.

Chad found his father's calm absolutely unsettling. 'This is crazy. Our own father is willing to help us dig up criminal evidence on the president of the university?'

'I say we go get changed and think of how we're going to get into the back.'

Mac came downstairs a few minutes later, dressed in a

207

navy blue sweat suit she'd found up in her room. Chad was in black sweat pants and a dark gray turtleneck. 'We look like we're in some B movie about a jewel heist,' he said, when he looked up and saw his sister. 'A B movie with a rotten costume designer.'

'What are you doing,' Mac asked as she stepped alongside his chair. He was working on a rough drawing with a heavy black pencil.

'Trying to remember the layout of Hutchinson's house in back. The ballroom extends further back than the rest of the house,' he said, elongating the rectangle on the left side of the drawing, 'Next to that is the garden room where we were. Is there a door there? I can't remember.'

'I don't think so. The back walls are all glass and I don't remember a door breaking up the wall.'

'Okay. The far right side is the pantry, and next to that is sort of a utility room. I think that's where we try to get in. If Phillip is like most people in Registon, he never locks the back door, except maybe at night.'

'Speaking of night, the sun's going to be down in about an hour, so I think we need to get a move on.'

They found their father in his office, and he noticed their change of clothing immediately. 'All set, are we?' He got up, tapped his pipe out into the ashtray that sat on his desk and started down the hall to the kitchen. He stopped, then called softly to his wife in her adjoining study. 'Elizabeth, I'm taking Mackenzie and Chadwick on an errand. We shouldn't be long.'

Walking to the kitchen, he said over his shoulder, 'I don't like keeping things from her, but I don't want her to worry

Now, tell me, about how much time do you think you'll need?'

Chad looked at Mackenzie, who shrugged her shoulders. 'A half-hour? But you're just going to drop us off, right, Dad? I mean, you don't have to wait for us to get out. Don't worry about it.'

'But I will worry. I can understand why you'd need a half-hour, perhaps even an hour, but if you aren't out of there in a reasonable time—'

'Let's not even worry about that, Dad,' Mac interrupted. 'Getting out usually isn't the problem, or so I've been told. Getting in is the big deal.'

THIRTEEN

Walker Griffin first drove beyond the Hutchinson driveway, and let them off at the property line that framed the north border of the Hutchinson land. The land was still heavily wooded here, so they could work their way up towards the house without being seen.

Before they ran across the lawn to the house, they knew they had to wait for their father's car to pull up the driveway, then a few moments more for him to get to the door. 'Mac, do you see what we're doing?' Chad said. 'We're actually hiding in the woods about to sneak into Avery Hutchinson's house.'

'Unbelievable, I know. And I was even lousy at hide-and-seek when we were kids, since my bladder seems to be the emotional center of my body at times like this.' Mac was half-joking, but she could feel herself getting tense.

'So we just go in, see if the collection we think is there is there, and, if it is, we get out and call Karlman, right?'

Mac nodded her agreement.

'That ought to be an interesting conversation,' Chad said, 'trying to get Karlman up to speed on this development.'

Mac started to move and realized she'd caught her sleeve on one of the prickly branches nearby. Trying to free herself, she scratched her cheek on another branch. 'Ouch! Dammit!' she said.

Chad looked at her, eyebrows arched in comment.

'I'm nervous. My language deteriorates when I'm nervous.'

At the point when they figured Phillip would be answering the door, they dashed across the rear lawn that sloped so beautifully and so gradually toward the river.

Chad tried the door to the utility room. He was right. It was open. They stepped inside, closed the door gently behind them and edged their way toward the hallway that ran alongside the kitchen and pantry. They could hear Phillip's voice, and that of their father.

' . . . absolutely foolish of me, of course,' their father was saying. 'He was kind enough to call yesterday to let me know that the meeting had been moved, and here I am showing up at the wrong time and disturbing you.'

'No disturbance at all, sir,' Phillip replied.

'What time did you say he'd be back?'

'I'm not certain of the exact time, sir, but he did say it would be later this evening.'

The walls of the hallway Chad and Mac were in were fairly straight on both sides, but the interior side was dominated by the curve of the staircase that formed part of the ceiling in the hallway. Chad looked up, pointed it out to Mac as though he saw some great significance in it. Mac shrugged her shoulders, since she wasn't sure what he was referring to.

They heard Phillip saying good-bye to their father, and they pressed close to the wall, hidden by the shadows cast by the large staircase, as he walked back through to the kitchen. He seemed to pause in there, and then they heard him ascending the back stairs. They waited another few moments, and then the sound of a television could be heard faintly. Chad listened to it intently. 'Football,' he whispered to his sister.

He indicated that he was going to lead the way, and, to Mac's surprise, he walked around in front of the huge staircase, to the hallway that mirrored the one they'd just come from. Chad was obviously looking under the curve of the ceiling, and he started feeling along the wall.

'What in the world are you looking for?' Mac asked, still whispering. 'I thought we agreed we were going to start downstairs in the basement.'

'As we were standing over there I remembered it. The hidden room. Underneath the staircase.'

Mac's eyes widened. 'The Underground Railroad room! Of course!' She peeked around to look at the front of the stairs. The stairways curved toward one another, but the bottom steps were at least six feet apart. In the space created by the curves of the two staircases, two curved benches, obviously built to fit the space, sat on either side; a wall that dropped down from the balcony/landing overhead created the rear of the space, and a beautiful gilt-framed oval mirror was placed in the center of the wall, hanging over a rectangular claw-footed table on which sat an arrangement of fall flowers. 'It's supposed to be underneath the landing, right?' she whispered.

'Yeah. I'm pretty sure,' Chad whispered back. 'I just can't figure out how you get into it.'

They worked their way back along the hallway, Chad feeling the wall with every step. The hallway led them into the garden room, the room where they'd been served cocktails and *hors d'oeuvres* exactly two weeks ago tonight. And here they were back so soon, Mac thought, only this time dressed as cat burglars.

Part of the interior wall of the garden room, the part that would have squared off with the hallway if it weren't for the door, was covered in wide white planking, a decorator's contribution to the rustic feel the garden room was supposed to have. Chad kept feeling around the wall and tapping. He tapped in the same place a few times, then directed a 'Pssst' at Mac to get her attention. She immediately stepped next to him.

'Hear this?' he said, tapping softly.

It did sound quite hollow to Mac's ears. 'Maybe it's just the planks over the wall. Wouldn't that make a hollow sound?'

'Not this hollow,' he replied, and started looking around to see if there was any way this wall opened. He crouched down and spotted some very discreet tracks in the masonry that rimmed the brick floor of the garden room. 'Look at this, Mac; there must be sections of this that move.'

He got up to inspect the tops of the planks, and, although they were well above his head, he saw shallow metal tracks up there as well. Figuring out what sections had to move to fit the tracks, he started placing his hands on the planks appropriately and giving a slight tug. After three tries, he was successful. Mac's eyes widened as a three-plank section of wall moved out of the way. Chad leaned inside the darkness, looking for and then feeling for a light switch. He found a circular one, a dimmer switch. He depressed it and the room inside came alive. He stepped in, guided Mac inside ahead of him, and closed the panels behind them.

'Chad, would you look at this place?' Mackenzie said. The room looked square, about fifteen by fifteen, and it was carpeted in a rich, deep blue. The walls were paneled in wood, in an old style of paneling that Mac recognized from some of the houses in town that were built in the early nineteenth century. At intervals along the paneling on three walls visible to them paintings were hung, each beautifully lit from sources that were hidden in the ceiling. The wall to their back, where the door to the garden room was, had paneled doors that led to a small, shallow enclosed area with shelves along the wall. It had probably been a closet at some point. Closets in these old homes were notoriously shallow.

In between the paintings, Mac noticed, sat exquisite display cases. The cases all had beautiful curved wooden legs in what looked to be some kind of fruitwood, and the tops were covered in glass or plexiglass – it was difficult to tell. The cases were lined in a deep blue velvet that almost matched the color of the carpet, and the material had been artfully arranged so that the objects displayed seemed cushioned in its folds.

Chad walked toward the first case on the left and let out a long, slow whistle. 'Would you look at these things, and the way they're displayed. There's even a notation next to each item!'

Mac saw that the first display case held what looked to be a large clay fragment of some kind. It was substantial in size, probably eighteen inches from top to bottom and twelve to fifteen inches in its jagged width. There were rough edges all around. The scene that was painted on it was faded in color, and showed an older man walking, gesturing with his hands, and three younger men surrounding him. 'What is it?' Mac said, when she saw Chad bending down to read the card. ' "Wall panel, Greece, presumed first century B.C. Believed to be the first pictorial depiction of Plato's Academy." ' He stood up quickly and looked in his sister's direction. 'Do you think that could be true?'

Mac had moved behind and around him to the next object on display. 'Look at this, Chad. It's another painting of Plato's Academy, or so it says,' she said, staring at the text underneath the frame.

'Yeah, that's the typical Renaissance style,' he said, looking at the flowing robes, the classic profiles depicted. 'They went totally apeshit over the Greeks.'

Mac frowned at his choice of words. 'Sorry, I lost my head,' he apologized.

Mac moved on to the next case. 'This looks like a coin,' she said. 'But it's big, and it looks like it would be heavy.'

'Can you see what it reads?' Chad said as he walked around to read the descriptive card. The two of them hit on the same words at once. 'Oh my God, this says Julius Caesar,' Mac said as Chad read off the accompanying card, ' "Commemorative coin struck in celebration of Julius Caesar's return to Rome. 46 B.C." '

They looked at each other, dumbfounded. 'Where did he

get this stuff?' Chad said. 'Tell me Malcolm Howard was *this* connected.'

Mac turned to the display case that was directly behind her. The display here was a hand-written manuscript on very old paper, four pages only. She recognized the style of writing from the many copies of historical documents her father had kept in his office over the years. Once she got the 'f's and 's's straightened out, Mac had enjoyed reading those documents and their language flavored with another time, and she leaned over to see how much of this one she could make out. 'No,' she whispered almost as soon as she began reading, 'not possible.'

'What?' Chad joined her.

' "When in the course of human events," ' she read, ' "it becomes necessary for a people to advance from that subordination in which they have hitherto remained, and to assume among the powers of the earth the equal and independent station to which the laws of nature and of nature's god entitle them, a decent respect to the opinions of mankind requires that they should declare the causes which impel them to the change. We hold these truths to be sacred and undeniable; that all men are created equal and independent, that from that equal creation they derive rights inherent and inalienable, among which are the preservation of life, and liberty, and the pursuit of happiness . . ." '

'The Declaration of Independence?' Chad said. 'Come on!'

'Jefferson's complete draft before submitting it to the Congress, it says,' Mac responded, looking up from the card. 'It's a good thing Dad didn't come with us. We'd never get him away from here.' She resumed reading the document.

'Look, Chad,' she whispered after a few moments. 'Jefferson got mixed up on the use of "its".'

'What do you mean?'

'He uses the apostrophe where it isn't needed. Down here. "Laying it's" – apostrophe s – "foundations on such principles and organizing it's" – apostrophe s – "powers in such form . . ." '

'Thomas Jefferson making a grammatical error?' Chad said. 'Hard to believe.'

'I think it's sort of sweet. Makes him more human, in a way.' Something in the next case caught her eye. 'What's that drawing there?' she said, pointing it out to her brother.

' "Fulton's Notes on Propelling a Boat by Steam Power 1804," ' Chad read. 'I see we finally made it to the Industrial Revolution.'

'You know, that collection of things in New London is suddenly making sense.'

'How do you mean?'

'It's like those things were the runners-up. The runners-up. Whatever. Who wants a weight marking the fifteenth anniversary of some second-rank Roman emperor when you have the coin commemorating Julius Caesar? Who needs a bunch of Greek vases, when you have the first depiction of Plato? What's that?' Mac said, suddenly turning her head to the door and wishing she had been whispering more softly.

They both listened intently, and they heard footsteps heading down the hall to the garden room. Mac's eye widened in alarm, as did Chad's, and they both moved as quickly as they could, as silently as they could, back to the door where they'd entered. Somebody was moving the plank panels on the other side! Mac slapped her hand over her mouth, eyes huge. Chad quickly turned out the light and they both slipped into the small closet. The closet was shallow enough that Mac had to take a couple of quick sidesteps to make room for Chad. He managed to quietly pull the sliding door across to hide them just as the other door opened.

'I think you'll find this fascinating,' a voice said. It was President Hutchinson's voice they heard. 'It's a most interesting collection, if I do say so myself.'

'Pretty impressive room,' another man's voice said. 'Mind if I take a look around?'

'No, of course not.' President Hutchinson sounded uncharacteristically nervous. Mackenzie tried to remember if she'd ever seen the man ruffled. If she had, she couldn't remember it.

'This some kinda prayer book?' the other man's voice said.

'Yes, it's an illuminated manuscript from a monastery in Britain. Tenth century. I've been given to understand that the level of artistry is almost equal to the Book of Kells.'

A few moments of silence and a few footfalls.

'This a blueprint kind of a thing?'

'Yes, it's a drawing of the plan for part of the cathedral at Chartres.'

Another few steps. 'This map here, what is it?'

'That's New England,' Hutchinson replied. 'In fact,' his voice grew muffled as he obviously stepped very near the wall, 'here's the Connecticut River, which you can see from that room we just left.'

219

'So this is Long Island here? How come it's running this way?'

'It wasn't until after this map was done that the convention of north always being at the top was adopted. They gave the center of the map over to whatever they wanted to detail the most. Here you see there's quite a bit of detail on Cape Cod. Martha's Vineyard. Nantucket. Over here is Block Island.'

'Interesting. Very interesting.'

'I had an extraordinary map, a beautifully colored one that purported to be a fifteenth-century map of the known world, notably without North and South America. But it turned out to be a nineteenth-century copy.'

Chad turned to Mac and winked an exaggerated wink.

'So where you gonna put the belt?'

Chad nudged Mac. Their eyes, accustomed to the dark by now, caught and held, growing wider with every sentence they heard.

'The belt will go right here, in the next case,' Hutchinson replied. 'In fact, if you'd like to show it to me, I'll put it in the case while you're here.'

They heard something set down with a clank, and then the sound of metal moving across metal.

'Look at it!' Hutchinson said reverently. 'It's exquisite!'

'You said this was called the Belt of the . . .' The man obviously didn't know the rest of the term.

'Conqueror. It's the Belt of the Conqueror.'

'So who's the conqueror?'

'Cortes. When he marched into Tenochtitlan in 1519, there are depictions both by the Spaniards who kept journals of their voyage, and in some Aztec drawings as well, of Montezuma greeting him and offering a gift of some kind. In one of the Aztec drawings it appears as a metal belt. For years, maybe hundreds of years, rumors have circulated about it. A belt of solid gold. That makes sense, since that region had access to so much gold.'

On the words 'solid gold' Mac and Chad turned to one another again, still wide-eyed.

From the noise, it sounded like Hutchinson was spreading the belt out on the blue velvet fabric. 'Ancient gold like this,' he was saying, 'has a deeper tone than we're used to. Like it's been burnished with fire rather than sunlight.' He paused. 'What you are seeing is the last of an amazing empire that was here in North America. Magnificent, isn't it?'

'Yeah, real nice,' the other man said. 'Look, I'm glad we were able to help you out on this one. Sorry it took so long. And sorry it got messy.'

Mac started to relax. It sounded like they were going to leave.

'Yes,' said Hutchinson, closing the display case. 'I don't know what happened with Howard. He seemed to have lost all control over this. I'm still astounded that he pulled a gun on your man, though.'

'Hey, from what my boys told me, he was ready to protect this thing with his life.'

Mac tried not to breathe. They were nearing the door to the garden room. Then she realized with some dread that she was going to sneeze, and sneeze loudly. However, she had developed an ability over the years to contain her sneezes. She put her hand over the mask of her face and was able to minimize it to an almost inaudible 'achoo'. Unfortunately, in reaching her hand up to her face, her elbow hit a light switch on the front wall of the closet, a 'soft-touch' switch she hadn't even noticed. She and Chad were now brightly illuminated inside the small closet. And the sliding door had been left slightly ajar, so a bright ribbon of light fell across the dark blue carpet. Even more light spilled out when President Hutchinson shoved aside the sliding door, as he did within seconds.

It was hard to tell who was the more startled – Mackenzie, or Chad, or Hutchinson and the man who now stepped into Mackenzie's line of vision. The man she immediately recognized from the night before. Gianni di Luca. Mr Lucky.

'Oh, *shit*,' Mac said, not quite under her breath.

'Mackenzie,' Chad said quietly. 'I've been meaning to talk to you about your language.'

FOURTEEN

Walker Griffin had parked his car not far from the Hutchinson driveway on River Road, hoping to see his children come barreling out of the woods. He was surprised when he saw instead an unfamiliar car pulling into the driveway with Avery Hutchinson in the back seat. He considered what to do for the next few minutes, then got out of the car and started walking up the driveway.

'Griffin! Mackenzie! What's the meaning of this?' Hutchinson demanded, pulling them out into the room.

'We might well ask you the same question, sir,' Mac replied. 'What's the meaning of this?' She indicated the whole room and its collection with a tilt of her jaw.

'What's going on here? Who are these two?' di Luca said, obviously not thrilled with their presence.

'Chadwick Griffin and his sister Mackenzie. Both former students. And their parents are part of my faculty.'

'Tell him I'm also the new owner of the River's End Gallery, sir. The guy his "boys" beat the crap out of two weeks ago. Just a few days before they assaulted my sister in an elevator at her school.'

Hutchinson looked puzzled at first, and then the meaning of what Chad had just said seemed to filter into his brain. He turned to di Luca. 'Is this true? Your men have been assaulting people?'

'Phillip, I'm so sorry to bother you again,' Walker Griffin was saying. 'But my car seems to have died a short ways up on River Road. Would you mind if I called the garage?'

'Not at all, sir,' the butler replied. 'Right this way.' Phillip led him to the phone in the main parlor, to the right of the large entrance hall. 'I'll let myself out, Phillip. I've troubled you enough.'

'No trouble, sir. Excuse me.'

Griffin waited until he saw the butler disappear into the kitchen, then he peered around the archway, listening intently. He heard a muffled voice, then another, but he wasn't sure where they were emanating from.

'Sometimes things don't go so smooth, y'know,' di Luca replied to Hutchinson's accusatory question. 'The boys gotta improvise.'

'Improvise?' Mackenzie said. 'Is that what happened when your men killed Paul Noble out in Tulsa?'

'Killed? Who was killed?' said Hutchinson, turning his head as though he hadn't heard correctly. 'Paul Noble, did you say? The boy who graduated four, five years ago?'

'He's the one,' Chad said. 'He was the victim of a hit and run two days before Malcolm Howard died. A very suspicious hit and run.'

'And let's not forget Randy Toffmeyer out in Seattle. Another hit and run,' Mac added.

'Oh, dear Lord,' Hutchinson cried. 'This is inconceivable.'

Walker Griffin's conviction that he had to do something – anything – to assist his children in getting out of there had solidified when he passed the car sitting in front of the Hutchinson entrance. The two occupants had tried to stare him down. He knew instinctively, looking at them, that they were thugs. Well dressed, perhaps, but thugs nevertheless. And their presence there did not bode well for his children. Perhaps not even for Avery Hutchinson himself. He picked up the phone and dialed.

'Do you mean to tell me that your men killed not only Malcolm Howard but two other young men as well? What possible reason could they give for that?'

'You said to me and I said to them that you wanted the belt Howard had got for you, you wanted it kept discreet, like no one should know that you have it. This kid in Oklahoma was the one who did the deal for Howard to get the belt from the guy in Belize. That seemed like an open end, so the boys took care of him. To be discreet, like you said.'

Hutchinson looked horrified. 'Discreet? You killed a young man on the *chance* he might say something? To be discreet? Oh, God, this is grotesque.'

Di Luca was getting pissed off with Hutchinson, that was evident. His expression of disgust suddenly changed when they all heard several loud *pops*! Somewhere close by, guns were being fired. Di Luca reached under his jacket.

Karlman didn't know what to make of the call when he got it. The dispatcher told him it was Dr Walker Griffin, insisting that he be put through directly to the Chief.

Karlman had been planning to knock off soon, since it was pretty late on Saturday afternoon, but he decided to take the call. It never hurt to be accommodating to one of the town's leading citizens. And he had forgotten to get back to Griffin junior this afternoon.

'Chief Karlman? Walker Griffin here. I think you'd best get over to the Hutchinson house right away. There are two unsavory characters sitting in a parked car in front of the house, and I'm not sure what they've done with Hutchinson. I'd bring another officer if I were you.'

Karlman started to ask a question, but the line went dead. He radioed Henson to meet him on River Road, fast, but lay off the sirens and lights. If there was two guys sitting there, no reason to advertise that you're comin'.

He pulled onto the shoulder of River Road south of the Hutchinson driveway, out of sight of the house. In less than a minute, Henson approached from the north. Karlman spoke softly into the radio. 'We'll just drive up nice and calm and see what's going on, okay? But be prepared.'

They pulled up behind the Cadillac, Karlman's car first, leaving a full car's length behind the Caddy. The two police officers got out of their cars and started to approach the suspect car on either side. They hadn't yet cleared the rear bumper when Karlman saw the guy on the passenger side

226

pull out a gun. At the same instant, the driver's door started to open.

'Take cover!' Karlman shouted as he hit the gravel driveway and rolled behind the car. The sound of bullets whistled in the air, and patches of gravel exploded near them.

This was it. They finally found the fucking thing the other day; it was in the gallery all along. But part of the reason they'd finally found it was that Sonny had gone to the old man and begged – actually got down on his knees and begged – that Buster not go with him. 'Let me take Michael with me.'

'Michael? You mean young Michael?'

'Yes. He's ready. And he's got some patience to him, more than this Buster guy, and I think that's what this is going to take.'

The old man finally agreed. And he was right, too. Patience finally paid off.

They didn't have any trouble getting in, since the painters' uniforms worked like they usually did, and they'd even had plenty of time once they got in. They'd started tearing out things from the back, but they'd caught a piece of luck when they found it just outside the back hallway.

But now Buster was even more pissed at him than usual. He decided that the fact that Sonny had found the belt without Buster being there made him – Buster – look bad. Which was probably right. But at this point Sonny didn't give a rat's ass. After today, somebody else was gonna get stuck with this one. The old man had promised him.

And today it would be over. It was Thursday when they'd

found the belt. The old man had wanted to see it for himself first, and then yesterday they drove into the city so he could tell his friend in person that the favor was done. But delivery was another matter, and the old man was playing that to the hilt. Even though Mr Lucky's friend had been in the back seat on the drive up from the city, the belt stayed in the old man's hands the whole ride. Once he came back out, it would finally be over.

Buster was slumped on the passenger side, quieter than usual, still pissed as hell. Suddenly he turned his head slightly and stared into the side mirror. 'Well, whatta we got here? Finally a little action in this place!'

Sonny looked into the rearview mirror to see the police car pull up. No skin off his nose. They weren't doin' nothing, and as far as he knew the Connecticut state cops didn't have anything on him. That's why he couldn't fuckin' *believe* it when he saw Buster actually pull a goddamned gun out. Pullin' a gun on cops for no reason was maybe the stupidest thing in the world to do. He figured he was meat if he stayed in the car, so he opened the door to roll out to the side.

Mac's assessment of the situation deteriorated when she saw di Luca pull out a gun. Only moments before she'd been figuring how she and Chad could subdue this elderly gentlemen with no problem. Then she remembered how guns in the Old West had sometimes been called equalizers. How apropos. The gun she was staring at had suddenly made this probable septuagenarian more than equal to two strong, healthy people whose ages added together didn't equal his. Equalizer indeed.

Hutchinson, still distraught over the news he had heard, was disoriented by the sound of gunfire. 'What is that?' he said, quizzing Mac and Chad. It wasn't until he turned toward di Luca again that he saw the gun. 'Oh, for God's sake, man,' he said in his best professorial voice. 'Put that thing down.' His last words were accompanied by a slight shove which, given di Luca's age, was just enough to throw him off balance.

Both Chad and Mac saw the opportunity at the same instant and they rushed him. Chad pulled di Luca to the side while Mac grabbed his arm and thrust it up high, trying to neutralize the gun. Chad's strength was a little much for the old man, however, and he crumpled to the floor. His arm was still upraised as he fell, and the gun discharged as he hit the floor. The sound of glass breaking was very loud.

'Son of a bitch!' Karlman said, holding his left arm near his chest. A bullet had grazed him just above the elbow. 'You got cuffs on botha them?' he said to Henson.

Henson, red-faced and sweating in the autumn chill, nodded in the affirmative. He'd be reliving the last few minutes for a long, long time. He'd been on the passenger side of the cars when Karlman gave the call to drop, but he managed to get his gun out of the holster before he hit the ground. When the guy on the passenger side got out, Henson had a clear shot underneath the car right at the guy's ankles, and he took it. The guy went down like a load of bricks, and his gun fell underneath the front wheel.

By that time, the other guy was shooting it out with the Chief, him at the left front bumper of the car, the Chief at the left rear bumper. The guy winged the Chief, and that's when Henson stepped around the side and got the drop on him.

All in all, a pretty good afternoon. But, hell, if he'd wanted action like this, he'd've stayed in Hartford.

Walker Griffin was almost faint with relief when he saw his children walk into the hallway from the garden room. He'd heard a shot inside the house as well as the barrage of bullets outside. Phillip had come running from the kitchen, near to panic, but Griffin had kept him from opening the front door.

Chad was guiding Gianni di Luca by the arm, and Mackenzie walked alongside a defeated-looking Avery Hutchinson.

Walker decided that any questions he had would wait until they got home.

FIFTEEN

Mac didn't get her wish to sleep in on Sunday morning, either. Chief Karlman was at the house by eight o'clock and by ten the state police were there, too.

Karlman hadn't taken President Hutchinson into custody Saturday afternoon. He'd had his hands full with the other three. But he instructed Hutchinson not to leave his house. He hadn't.

After Karlman and the state-police detective heard Chad and Mac recount their two weeks of digging, the state detective, Eric Telfair, said, 'You two did this all on your own?' He glared at Karlman accusingly while asking the question. Karlman didn't notice.

'No, we had some help,' Mac said. She gave him the names of Buratti, Jarvi, and Daly, the FBI agent. 'You might want to get in touch with them tomorrow morning.'

Just before noon, Mac excused herself from the dining room where they'd been answering questions for hours. She reappeared a few minutes later, clothes changed, bag thrown over shoulder. 'Can I have to keys to the rental car, Chad?' she said.

'You're leaving?' he said as he stood up. His question was echoed by the other two men at the table.

'You bet. I'm going to get on the road before Sunday traffic builds up, I'm going to return the car, and then I'm going to go home and *sleep.*' She looked at the officers. 'Gentlemen, if you need to reach me, my brother can give you my various numbers.' She headed for the kitchen door. Chad followed.

'I said good-bye to Mother and Dad already, so give me a hug, little brother, and let me get out of here.'

Chad put his arms around her and squeezed. 'What can I say, Mackenzie? I wouldn't have made it through the last two weeks without you.'

'Damn straight you wouldn't have,' she said and then winked at his reaction. 'Gotcha.'

'Bye, Stella,' she said, kissing the older woman on the cheek as she passed. 'See you at Thanksgiving if not before.'

'Are you sure you won't be staying for dinner, Mackenzie? The pork loin looks splendid.'

'And I'm sure it will taste even better, Stella. But this is one of those rare times in life that not even your cooking can tempt me away from my pillow. 'Bye,' she said again and was out the door.

She poked her head back in seconds later and called for Chad. 'Be sure you call Tom Vandeveere and let them know that it's okay for Beth to leave.' Chad shooed her away saying he'd take care of it.

Traffic was light, and she made it to Manhattan in very good time. By the time she turned in the rental car and cabbed it home, it was 2:45. By the time her head hit the pillow, it was 2:50.

The phone rang just before seven. Luckily, she'd come out of her deep sleep and had just been dozing for the last half-hour or so. Recreational sleeping, as she called it.

It was Peter on the phone. 'Mackenzie? Is that you? It's your real, live voice?'

'Peter, how are you?' she said, sitting up in bed. 'Where are you?'

'Auckland, New Zealand. Did I wake you up? What time is it there? Better yet, what day is it there? They told me it was seventeen hours difference between here and New York and I got seasick trying to figure the time.'

'Don't worry about it,' she said softly. 'Tell me about New Zealand. What's it like?'

'Beautiful, what I've seen. But disorienting. It's spring here. It's the end of November and it's spring.'

'That's right. It would be. And how have the concerts been going?'

'Just fabulous,' he said. 'The audiences are amazing. I've got so much to tell you. But what's with this New Mexico thing? What kind of investigation are you working on with your brother?'

'It's too long a story. I'll tell you when you get back. When is that, by the way?'

'Thanksgiving Day. They added some dates and some press interviews, so we're not leaving Australia until a week from Tuesday. Are you going to be up with your family on Thanksgiving?'

'During the day, yes. But I can arrange to be back here by early evening.'

'Good. I'm due into Kennedy at noon, and I'll stop and see my family. Then I'll have a car bring me into the city.' He was silent for a moment. 'I can't wait to see you, Mac.'

'Me, too. It'll be good to have you home.'

She didn't realize what she'd said until after she'd hung up the phone. Were she and Peter, together, becoming her new definition of 'home'?

News kept dribbling in from Chad for the next ten days. The news early in the week was good. There had been some kind of legal determination, after a review of the gallery sale documents and Malcolm Howard's will, that Chad, as proprietor of River's End Gallery, was indeed the owner of the goods stored in unit 113 of Old Colony Storage in New London.

Everyone involved was quite certain there would be no protest, since Malcolm Howard had died with no family or heirs. The sole beneficiary of his estate was Riverside University. 'Ironic, isn't it?' said Chad when he reported that particular fact.

More good news followed. Almost the entire Greek and Roman collection was sold to the two dealers Tom Vandeveere had referred Chad to. Papers on virtually all of the pieces had been found in Malcolm Howard's personal records; it turned out that the entire collection was authentic. Chad insisted that his mother have a choice of any two pieces she wanted from the group, however. And for himself he kept the head of Dionysus.

'All those pieces were – are – real?' Mackenzie said when Chad told her the news. 'What were they doing in storage in New London?'

'Apparently Malcolm was counting on some end-of-the-millennium boom, and hoping the prices would go up. So I guess you could say he was hoarding.'

Most of the paintings were genuine as well, to the surprise of almost everyone involved. Malcolm Howard had been tempted over to 'the dark side' as Chad referred to it, and in the last ten years he'd helped to place Riverside grads in jobs in key museums across the country. He was able to pull off the switches he had – replacing originals with very good forgeries – precisely for the reasons Jarvi had stated. Malcolm Howard didn't pull switches on the high profile 'masterpieces'. He went after the second-tier works.

Two of the paintings in the storage were those that Angelo Campanelli had arranged for the 'security duplicates' on, the term he kept insisting on using during the course of the investigation. Campanelli's fate was still undetermined.

More good news had followed later in the week. Good news of a kind, that is. It turned out that Randy Toffmeyer's death was unrelated to the other events. He had in fact died in a traffic accident. The Seattle police had finally picked up the driver who had hit and run. That was some comfort at least to Avery Hutchinson, who was now free on bail after spending a night in the New London county jail. He had not been seen outside his home since.

The dream that had begun when Avery Hutchinson's beloved wife was still with him was no more. The dream of a

Hutchinson Collection on Western Civilization, an unparalleled gathering of the finest emblems and artifacts. The collection would have been presented to Riverside University on his retirement, or at his death; that was a detail he hadn't decided as yet. Either way, it would be a glorious swan song for his family, one that would insure their name would continue.

For he was the last of the Hutchinsons. Oh, there were a few distant cousins, but the true Hutchinsons of Registon line died with him. Going back three generations, each father had produced only one son. And then he'd had none.

Hutchinson's grandiose dream had turned into a tragi-comic grotesquerie of thefts, muggings, petty hoodlums, and even murder. And the Hutchinson name, his proudest asset, was not only muddied, he was now the subject of ridicule and ghastly jokes. He wasn't certain he could bear the pain.

Mackenzie finally got more of the lowdown when she made it back up to Registon the day before Thanksgiving.

'Avery Hutchinson finally came clean,' Chad told her as they heated some cider, trying to stay out of Stella's way. The day before Thanksgiving was not the day to cross this woman.

'Came clean how?'

'Came clean with the story on what happened to Malcolm Howard. It seems Howard had been "procuring" things for him for a couple of years. It sounds like it was almost a mutual blackmail pact, but who knows who got dirty first. But apparently when Howard realized what they had on hand with the Belt of the Conqueror, or what he thought they had on, he bolted. He told Hutchinson it was wrong for this to stay in private hands, that something like this belongs to the ages, which I guess meant it belongs in a museum. This was all going on when we were wrapping up the sale on the gallery and it's apparently the reason Malcolm was so secretive about the sale.

'In fact, Hutchinson didn't find out about Malcolm selling out to me until that week before Halloween, and that was when he started putting the pressure on, because he knew Malcolm had or would shortly have the belt in his possession. He and Malcolm got into a few good screaming matches, and when he thought Howard was going to fold his tent and disappear into the night with the Belt of the Conqueror in hand, that's when Hutchinson called Mr Lucky, who had previously offered his services. Hutchinson swears that he was told they were taking Howard out on the boat only to scare him enough to make him cough up the belt – I guess Malcolm was terrified of the water – and then "the boys" came up with some bogus story about him pulling a gun on them.'

' "The boys"?'

'Yeah, the two guys who were out in front of Hutchinson's place, the two who jumped you, the two who got me in the gallery. Buster and Sonny, if you can believe. They had taken Malcolm out on the boat to scare him. But, now this is according to Sonny, Buster apparently has quite a temper on him. At some point Malcolm insulted Buster and the guy just point-blank shot him. Sonny was the one smart enough – if that's the term – to come up with the he-pulled-a-gun-on-us story for di Luca.'

237

'So Malcolm got killed for insulting this goon?' Mac said, shaking her head.

'He got killed for insulting a goon with a bad temper who had a gun in his hand. Not a prudent thing to do.'

Mackenzie tried to sip her cider, but it was still too hot to drink. 'The "he" in "he must be stopped" was Hutchinson, then, right?' she finally said.

'Seems so. It sounds like Malcolm Howard really got an attack of conscience over this whole thing.'

'And "His Lordship" was Hutchinson, too? Do we know why?'

'I specifically asked Detective Telfair to find out what that was all about. It seems that Sonny and Buster had cased out Hutchinson's home. And one of them said it looked just like the house in a movie his girlfriend had just dragged him to, one that he really hated. But the owner of the house in the movie was "His Lordship" and that's what he started calling Hutchinson, as a joke. It apparently really got on the other guy's nerves, from what Telfair said,'

'So this little joke sidetracked us for how long?' Mac said.

'Think about it,' said Chad. 'I guess it's one of the prices we have to pay for Merchant-Ivory films.'

Mac held her mug between her hands, trying to warm them. It was going to be a cold Thanksgiving. 'Two questions. One, you said what Malcolm Howard *thought* they had on hand. What's that all about?'

'Oh, that's right, you don't know about that yet. I referred the Connecticut state police to Tom Vandeveere, who referred them to one of those archaeometrists he was telling us about. It seems the Belt of the Conqueror is a fake.'

238

Mackenzie's jaw dropped.

'Oh, it's real gold,' her brother explained, 'and there's a lot of it, so it's worth something. But it's twentieth-century gold, probably from the late teens or early twenties.'

'So Mr Howard died in the cause of a phony artifact?' Mac said. 'That's sad.'

'What was the second question? You said you had two.'

'Has anybody figured out how Avery Hutchinson and Gianni di Luca got together? Talk about the odd couple!'

'They met at the opera, can you believe?' answered Chad. 'Box seats next to one another at the Met for the last two years. Di Luca offered his services, should Hutchinson ever need them. Hutchinson took him up on the offer.'

'Last question. Did Fulton's notes on the steam engine make it through getting the display case shot up?'

'Mostly,' Chad said. 'There's an interesting chunk out of the upper right corner now. But when this whole story gets out, it'll only increase its value.' He got up to go fix the fire. They were going to need one this evening. It was getting very chilly.

He pushed open the door to the dining room, then turned back. 'Mac, wait, there's one thing I forgot to tell you.'

'What?' she said, pouring some more cider.

'Tom Vandeveere called yesterday, asking about the dealers, the archaeometrists, all that stuff.'

'And?'

'He and Beth de Beaupre won't be celebrating Thanksgiving today, because they were flying down to Mexico – to get married.'

'*Married?*'

239

'Married.'

Mackenzie gave her brother an exaggerated grin. 'Well, I guess they were getting under one another's skin, but not quite the way I thought.'

They watched the parade Thanksgiving morning, and the mouth-watering aroma of roast turkey was already permeating the house by the time Santa arrived at 34th Street. Stella had been up since dawn, since they were having the usual large gathering, with some fifteen to eighteen guests expected. Some were relatives coming down from West Hartford, others were university colleagues of Walker and Elizabeth Griffin. Whitney was due in from Boston around noon. Mac hadn't seen her sister since the weekend after Labor Day and was looking forward to seeing her, however brief a visit it would be.

Mac and her mother were in the kitchen late morning, working on the one dish that Stella allowed them to be in charge of – the Waldorf salad. Elizabeth Griffin prided herself on the preparation of this salad, and made somewhat of a production out of it, since it was the only thing she'd ever prepared in a kitchen in her life. After the guests arrived, there was one inevitable moment when she would excuse herself, saying, 'I must see how the salad is coming along.'

Mackenzie had cut up the walnuts already. Chopping them wouldn't do, according to her mother; the walnuts must be hand-cut. They were almost finished with peeling and cutting the apples, but there were still all those grapes to be cut in half. Her mother had been giving a rundown of the expected guests, and had got to the end of the list. Or so it seemed.

'And Dad said you invited Doctor Houston,' she said, referring to her father's colleague whom she'd met at the Hutchinson party at the beginning of the month. The beginning of the month that now seemed like eons ago. 'That's nice. First Thanksgiving in New England and all. I'm sure he'll have a good time.'

'Yes, I'm sure he will. And your father and I thought that he and Chadwick might suit.'

Mackenzie paused mid-slice on her apple. For a moment there, she had thought it sounded like her parents were trying to fix Chad up. But that wasn't possible. For one thing, Mackenzie wasn't sure that her parents even knew that Chad was gay. For another, Walker and Elizabeth Griffin were the least likely matchmakers on earth. She couldn't even imagine a conversation between them in which the subject would come up. Her parents, after all, were people who seemed blithely oblivious to most everything in life except their studies. They seemed out of contact with most of the twentieth century, and had never expressed any interest in their children's social lives. These were the people, after all, who had asked Peter Rossellini what he thought of 'this Presley chap' as though Elvis were still alive.

Certainly this was one of those occasions when her ears were playing tricks on her. Or was it?

Mac kept her head down to the task at hand, but raised her eyes to look at her mother, Elizabeth Griffin caught her daughter's eye with a shrewd look Mackenzie didn't think she'd ever seen before. 'I'm not a complete turnip, my dear.'

Dear God, Mackenzie thought, were things *ever* what they seemed to be?

More Thrilling Fiction from Headline Feature

Emma Lorant

CRADLE OF SECRETS

HER DREAM OF TWINS TURNED INTO A NIGHTMARE

When Alex and Lisa Wildmore move to the pretty Somerset village of Lodsham, they anticipate a rural idyll. Newly pregnant, with one adorable toddler already, Lisa is confident that the countryside is the best place to raise her family; she embodies the good life of the caring 'nineties.

But the sun-dappled tranquillity of the Glastonbury moors is deceptive.

Childbirth brings identical twin boys, despite a scan showing only one baby. When it becomes clear that this is only the start of a terrifying chain of events she is powerless to prevent, Lisa realises she is in the grip of a phenomenon as sinister as it is inexplicable.

Of course she loves her children – blond, blue-eyed and enchanting – and is determined to protect them from any dangers that might attend their unusual genesis. And a rash of 'accidents' convinces Lisa that there are dangers indeed.

Whom can she trust with her cradle of secrets? Alec assumes she is suffering delusions brought on by post-natal depression. Previously friendly villagers adopt a hostile curiosity. Can she even trust her own maternal instincts? Or is Lisa Wildmore losing her mind . . . ?

FICTION / THRILLER 0 7472 4358 1

Joy Fielding

The Other Woman

'Excuse me, Mrs Plumley. I'm Nicole Clark. I'm going to marry your husband.'

At first, Jill thinks it's a joke. After all, it is her fourth wedding anniversary. And she and David are blissfully happy – aren't they? But the incident is unsettling. It starts her thinking. And she finds herself increasingly vulnerable.

Because Jill Plumley has been 'the other woman' in her husband's first marriage. She's heard David's excuses – working late at the office; weekends away on business – from the point of view of the demanding mistress. But now she's on the other side of the fence, those excuses have a horribly familiar ring.

Call it poetic justice or just bad luck. The fact is that again there's another woman in David Plumley's life: a young, pretty, sexy, ambitious woman who knows exactly what she wants – Jill's husband.

FICTION / GENERAL 0 7472 4435 9

DANGEROUS ATTACHMENTS

A silent watcher in the dark . . .

Sarah Lovett

Psychologist Sylvia Strange is called to New Mexico's male prison to evaluate a convicted murderer seeking parole. But, after deciding that Lucas Watson is seriously disturbed, she cannot recommend his release.

That's where her nightmare begins . . .

Watson is the son of an influential politician, and soon Sylvia finds herself exposed to personal harassment. At first she reckons that Lucas himself is somehow responsible – so when he is dramatically removed from the scene, surely her life will return to normal?

Except it doesn't.

All around her, events spin out of control. Her good friend Rosie, prison investigator, has to cope with a mythical inmate called 'the jackal' who hideously amputates body parts from other human beings – both dead and alive . . . A professional associate is bludgeoned to death in his bath tub . . . And Sylvia finds herself reluctantly attracted to a brash police officer.

As she struggles with her investigations through the bitter cold of a desert winter, a shocking tale of family secrets, obscene murder and diabolic obsession unfolds.

FICTION / THRILLER 0 7472 4616 5

More Compelling Fiction from Headline Feature

KATHERINE NEVILLE
A CALCULATED
RISK

Verity Banks is *the* senior woman executive at the Bank of the World, a
prestigious global financial institution: a top computer expert, she lives
and breathes the world of big money and big power. But when her boss
axes her proposal to improve the bank's computer security, Verity
decides to teach him a lesson.

She plans to break into the bank's computer system and hide some
money where no one will ever find it – within the system itself. Then she
can point out just how essential her new security proposals are. It all
seems simple – until the reappearance in Verity's well-ordered and
unemotional life of Dr Zoltan Tor.

Intense and mysterious, Tor is a financial wizard who taught his protégée
Verity everything about technology, commerce and the fine art of
sensual living. Now he is back with a challenge: which of them can
steal a billion dollars and invest it to earn thirty million in three months?
The prize: that the loser must grant the winner's dearest wish . . .

'Notable . . . there isn't a dull moment. It churns up wave after
wave of excitement' *New York Times*

'A first-rate page-turner, written with real intelligence'
Good Book Guide

'A richly complex and inventive story, stirring and exciting'
Susan Hill, *Good Housekeeping*

'The novel is brilliantly crafted and totally involving. I didn't
want to put it down for an instant' *Woman and Home*

'A feminist answer to *Raiders of the Lost Ark*' *Washington Post*

FICTION / GENERAL 0 7472 4071 X

A selection of bestsellers from Headline